I0637461

In Search of Aimai Cristen
By Phillip Good
56,000 words

1. The Ad

Young attractive girl, 24, searching for
love, compassion, joy from a man who can
provide financial security. Write Aimai
Cristen, Box 3689, Barb Office, 1234
University Ave, Berkeley CA 94709.

2. Dino

My dad and I have had our ups and downs over the years.

When we were younger, he spent a lot of time with my older sisters and not very much with me. He would play catch with them or challenge them to races, but "because Dina couldn't keep up," he wouldn't play those games when I was around or would announce he was "tired" when I came out to play.

This isn't quite true, Dana tells me. Dana says our family also had another game called "Roll the Ball." We'd sit in a circle with Dad at the center, our legs separated so as to make a 'V', and he'd take turns rolling the ball to each of us. Dana's got a photograph of the four of us sitting in a circle on the floor of our family room—the house back in Michigan; my back and Dad's back are to the camera, and Dad, still with his long dark hair, is rolling the ball to Dana, so I guess it must be true.

"And what about 'Sardines,' and 'Puss in the Corner'?" Dana would probably ask. And we did go cross-country skiing in the winter and swimming together as a family in the summer: "Marco Polo." O.K., but I still think Dad spent more time with Dana and Donna.

About two months ago, I came back home to live with my father. I'd dropped out of school for a while. Done some things I wasn't particularly proud of. I got a job when I was only sixteen: telephone soliciting. And I had a job with one of those 900 numbers—"Intimate secrets," my seductive voice promises, "What do girls really think about when they're alone? You can listen for just $2.35 a minute. Ten-minute minimum." But mostly my friends and I sat around in crummy apartments and talked. Talked all morning and all afternoon. Talked some more and partied in the evenings.

I came back home because I know now what I want to do. Go to college. Get a teaching credential. And work with kids that have problems. Of course, I have a few things to get out of the way first, like getting the high school diploma I never quite got around to completing.

Well, why not? I need just algebra and a semester of Spanish to get the diploma. It has to be done sometime. And like my dad always said, "you're bright enough."

Dana lived a year alone in the house with Dad in her last year of high school. (Never mind they no longer speak.) Now, it is my turn. (She says she came up to him once after a lecture he gave at her college and he looked right through her like she was a total stranger. He says he did try to talk to her, but her politics are so extreme she just won't listen to anybody. They're both partly right.)

Since I came back, Dad and I have been part of a tight domestic scene: Breakfast together in the mornings if I get up on time, dinner together in the evening. Nothing really special for dinner. Dad knows how to make spaghetti—he gets real excited because he uses fresh cheese and grates it at the table. I'll fix a salad or sometimes he'll have one already made. Dad also fixes roasts. He's very particular about how they are cooked; he steams the vegetables separately and only adds them to the meat at the very end. I know how to make stuffed peppers and almost any kind of dish where you start with rice and then stir in your leftovers. For dessert we both like ice cream.

I'm not sure what else we are supposed to do together, talk maybe?

"How are those math courses coming?" Dad will ask. He reaches up a hand and absent-mindedly scratches his scalp; I wish he wouldn't.

"O.K. I know most of the stuff... Seriously, I got A's in my last three assignments."

"I believe you. Seen this in the paper about the retards on the school board?"

"It's a shame." I reply, wondering why we aren't talking about anything meaningful.

He shakes his head, takes off his reading glasses and looks at me. I meet his gaze. Though his cropped hair is shot through with gray, his eyes are still dark and penetrating. "You've got to read the newspaper more, read books they don't assign you in class."

"O.K." I say to pacify him. And that's our evening's conversation. A wall sits between us, and I can't push through it, yet.

There isn't much to night school: a couple of evenings a week in the classroom with other lowlife dropouts, a couple of mornings doing the assignments and reading. College, I know, will be a lot harder. But right now, I'm left with a lot of time on my hands.

I don't need to work—at a job I mean. Dad says as long as I live at home and am going to school, he'll pay for everything. I'm not going to hang out—no, not for me, not any more, not with a bunch of guys going no place. (Though I might stop back to talk with them later, when I have my teaching credential.) So what do I do when I'm not in school? Stay at home? Go shopping at the mall?

When I moved in with my dad originally, I thought I'd be really domestic. Cook, clean, take care of everything for him. But he's learned a lot in the two years he was apart from Mom. He cleans up now as he goes along. You know, he wipes off counters and puts the dishes away in the dishwasher as soon as the meal is over. So there isn't much mess left for me to clean.

I could do the vacuuming—"I'll do that, Dad."—unless he's already done it himself. Our house is so small. Well, not small, small, but it seems tiny to me sometimes with Dad holed up in his study all day long and me tiptoeing around trying not to disturb him.

I've cleaned my own room a dozen times over. I've thought about putting up pictures but I haven't quite got around to it yet. Maybe, because I don't know who my heroes are, whose photos I want on my wall.

4

Which leaves me what: A chance to mow the grass (once Dad is through in his study and the noise won't bother him) or clean up the garage.

"It's a mess out here, Dad," I say, though I know he is inside in his study and can't hear me. Cobwebs and a wasp nest have to be cleaned up first. Lots of boxes, the same boxes he's lugged around with us since I was a kid. "Can I throw this out?" Children's clothing in a box marked "Give to Goodwill" years ago by my mom. After a parting squeeze for my last pair of Dr. Denton's, I put the box out on the curb and see that it goes off to Goodwill, finally.

A paper bag full of crumpled envelopes and computer printouts goes into the garbage where it belongs. Here is a second bag, this one filled with white Styrofoam pebbles —"Don't throw that out," Dad hollers, appearing from nowhere.

One box contains all the memos Dad wrote or had sent to him when he worked years ago for a pharmaceutical firm. Its contents include the minutes of the Technical Library Committee: "Janet Henderson has volunteered to look into the possibility of microfiche." I leaf through both the report from Janet Henderson and a caustic memo from my dad criticizing her report. Ah well, let him keep his memos a while longer.

At supper—the entire house smells of the garlic that went into the sauce—I asked him about the garage, "Dad, I've started looking into the boxes. All your old manuscripts and memos. Is it O.K.?"

A broad smile lights up his face, first the left side of his mouth, then the right, the smile extending finally past his dimple to the crinkles in the corners of his eyes. "Sure, it's O.K. I'm flattered. I guess that's maybe why I keep the stuff. In case one or the other of you kids might want to know what I was up to in the old days."

Is this a conversation? Not yet, but I think we are getting closer.

The next afternoon, I put aside the company memos—they are as boring now as they were then—and seek out the older boxes—the ones that are pre Dina, even pre mom. I found one box that is really old; the tape holding the cardboard together has almost rotted away. I sneeze each time I disturb the dust on the outer surface. At the top of the box is a book of course notes from McGill University: Calculus 223 is dedicated in my father's uneven handwriting to a Miss Jan Davenport. Four more course notebooks lie beneath the first, each dedicated to a different girl. And yellowed newspaper clippings: "Street Car Fares to Rise a Dime. Students Protest." Here is a page from the Sunday Book Review Section, 195_ something: "Too Many Penguins" reviewed by Phillip Good, Willingdon School, Age 10. Oh my goodness, little Phillip Good of Willingdon Elementary School, father-to-be of Dina Good, high school student in perpetuem. Little Phillip likes the book and is anxious to read something more by the same author.

I switch to a box of more recent vintage. The outside is water stained and the contents are partially but not completely faded: Letters from Uncle Steven in green ink, letters from Uncle Pete in an almost undecipherable ballpoint. Uncle Pete had been in the Peace Corps. I didn't know that. A collection of Dear John, oops, Dear Phil letters:

"Dear Phil. I cannot go with you to the concert tonight. I am sorry but..." "Phillip: I like you, but as I told you when we first met, I already have a commitment..." "Dear Mr. Good, my father says that only fast girls will accept..."

And, as if to offset these letters, a note that reads, "Phil. I don't understand why you haven't called. Please. Jan."

The note still holds a faint scent of lilacs and I press my nose against the writing.

But it is the next and largest box that is the real treasure trove. Psychedelic posters—notebook size—advertise concerts at the Fillmore Auditorium: The Grateful Dead, Clear Light, Big Brother and the Holding Company, Yveshenko reading from his own poetry. (Yveshenko sounds Russian: did they have translators?) I put on a pair of glasses with multi-faceted colored lenses, one side yellow, one side pink; through them, everything looks the way it did to Jeff Goldblum in *The Fly*. And then—but will I have time before supper to read them? —a dozen brown manila folders, each containing an ill-assorted mixture of newspaper clippings and manuscripts, letters to the editor, poems, three columns of want ads, parts of a diary. These clippings may have had an order once; perhaps each folder corresponded to a different year or a different six-month period, but now they are all mixed up.

"Has anyone else seen these, Dad?" I ask about the envelopes, meaning has one of my older sisters seen them.

It is spaghetti evening, smelling of garlic again and Parmesan cheese. Dad got out his razor before the meal so the dining room smells a little, too, of shaving soap and Aqua Velva.

"Oh, I've been through them a couple of times." Dad says, "And I tried to get your mother interested. Have you read any of the stuff?" He tries to appear casual in asking, but something, a restless movement of his fingers, gives his need for recognition away.

"Just bits and pieces," I remark, trying to act equally laid back. Actually, I hadn't read any of the manuscripts, yet. I'm still depending on conversation to give me the glimpses of him I need. "Something else I wanted to ask you, Dad: You have this collection of letters that are still in their original envelopes."

"The ones from Uncle Steve and Moo Grandma?"

"No, the letters I'm talking about aren't addressed to you. They're to an Aimai something or other."

He takes off his reading glasses. "Aimai Cristen." His voice is muffled. I wait for him to explain who Aimai Cristen is but he doesn't say anything more, just sits and stares off into the distance.

"O.K., if I look at them, too?" I ask.

He nods, still not speaking. I can't tell from the nod if he means, "sure, the letters would be a good place to start," or "sure, I can't stop you." O.K., Dad, keep your mysteries. I can be cool, too. For a while.

The next afternoon, I am back in the garage early with the contents of two of the boxes spread out around me. I've made a stack of the card-size posters to put up on my wall. My dad was a fan of the Jefferson Airplane and Big Brother and the Holding Company. So am I now, whoever they were.

A manila folder holds clippings from the Berkeley Barb; copies of this same newspaper, neatly folded, line the bottom of the box. I unfold the newspapers and read the articles, one by one. A number of the stories are outlined in red as if Dad were planning to cut them out. Articles by Number Six, the Grass Prophet, Shiva, and Peter Wood.

The folders also contain a number of short stories. The heroes are named Rafe or Peter or Jim, but I think they are really about episodes in my Dad's own life.

Stories, clippings, extracts from his diaries. It's hard to believe, I tell myself each afternoon I sit cross-legged on the floor of the garage reading: All of my father's life is there in the box. Like coming home, all I have to do is reach out and say, "Hi Dad."

3. The Replies

Dear Aimai:

My name is art gentry. I am 33 yeras old, live in stockton. I am divoirced, two chilkdren both boys. I have my own bussiness, I am tired of living alone. My hight is 5' 9", I am a member of the volunteer fire dept. My position in the comunity is on the up swing so to say. A woman with a warm and plesant personalty is needed. One who wold help me with my bussiness, and becum an escential part of my life.

As you can see my typing is terrible. A swift replky would be ppercaited, any nesssary arrangement to meet is heartly acceatable.

Western Union Telegram

IF YOU ARE A VIRGIN, CALL BILL CUMMINGS COLLECT AT 916 644-7156. LETTER TO FOLLOW

Dear Aimai:

You sound fairly interesting; I'm sure you'll find someone who thinks you're terribly interesting.

You shouldn't have much trouble finding someone to support you around here even without the ad. Parties are rather free and open, though I think you'll find too many otherwise interesting and hip people who like me are ridiculously self-centered. There's nothing wrong with self-enjoyment but too many people can sit all day at the table eating ice cream and never get sick.

I've found it fairly easy here to share my differences with others, rather than let them become blockades. I'm 24, also, bearded, athletic, and am given to most sexual activities except those involving pain and/or a lack of consent.

Now comes the interesting part. If you'd like to get together sometime and talk, even if you're doubtful of an eventual friendship, fine.

Anyway, reference time. To be sure I won't rape you, you may contact Charity Millar (red-haired, drug-oriented—I'm not married and could have screwed her, but declined because of her marriage, Catholic upbringing, now strictly non-Christian, unless changed recently. (Cristen and Christian, is there a connection?) Charity will vouch for my goodness/honesty. Call her at 555-3447 in SF.

Also Les Barber, 883-1991 office or 551-8339 home, a good friend of mine,

active with the Campus Crusade for Christ.
Two more distinguished and diversified
references would be hard to find. Anyhow,
I think my relationships with them mirror
what I said about sharing differences.

Tom

The next letter is stuck to the envelope and rips when I try to unfold it.

Dear Aimai:

I am a divorced male, early fifties. Shortly after I got married,
in my early twenties, I discovered my wife was not a virgin,
although she had told me she was. I put up with it for years
and divorced her finally.

Since then, I have met a number of women who said they
were virgins and were not.

If you are a virgin, I have plenty of money and am well able
to support you and give you all the things that you need.

If you are a virgin, call Bill Cummings collect at 916 644-
7156.

We had a fire going in the fireplace that evening. The weather was
just on the verge of being cold. I liked the fire as much or more for
the aroma of the burning wood as for the warmth.

Dad was grading papers. I'd rediscovered the box containing the
replies to Aimai Cristen's ad and had brought them inside from the
garage determined that Dad and I would have a meaningful
conversation. "How'd you get these letters, Dad?"

"She gave them to me."

I waited for him to say more, but he remained silent, ruminating about Aimai Cristen, perhaps, or merely deciding whether to give an extra half-point for an especially good answer.

"Can I read them?"

"Be my guest."

He smiled as if he knew a secret I didn't know. But he didn't say another word, then, about the letters.

Dear Miss Cristen:

Things haven't gone well since my wife left.

She took all the furniture. I use just the one room where the bed was and of course the kitchen to keep canned goods and such.

It is quite a large house but it is empty now. I usually don't stay in it much except when I sleep. It is very lonely. You probably won't want to write to me.

Dan

I thought about Dan's letter and decided I wouldn't have sent him a reply. A lot of my friends have gotten involved with guys like Dan, thinking, "He just needs motivation." It doesn't work. I want someone who believes in himself.

"Who would want to write to a guy this empty?" I say to my Dad.

"Mother Teresa, maybe. Or some girl who's decided to devote her life to healing the sick."

"Not me."

"Really? Is that why you learned sign language when you were thirteen?"

"That's work. And the deaf aren't pretending to be sick. 'Oh, it's so very lonely.' The deaf have got real physical problems. I can help them. This guy, you can't help."

A slow smile crept over my Dad's face. He looks really handsome when he smiles. "I agree with you. Dan would be the wrong guy for you, for any girl really. He says he's lonely, but it's really because he is totally into himself. If he wanted to meet somebody, he'd be out there looking—a bar, a grocery store, someplace. But he's at home, whining. The man you love should be capable of loving you in return."

"There isn't any self there," I said.

Dear Aimai:

You sound like a very interesting girl. I would like very much to meet you.

Let me tell you a little about myself. I am a Negro man, 32 years of age, 6'2" tall, weight around 165. I am not a professional man, but I am a business man. I have a number of business ventures going. As a matter of fact, too many, though I still find time for love.

I do not look for a wife as yet, but I would like to take you out some time. I don't care very much for night clubs, but I will drink a little with the girl I am with. I love to go to movies. I am a well-known business man around town. (If you have any talent in entertainment, tell me about it. I'll get you in the next big show I bring to town.)

I love to pick up my date and get out of town, like Sacramento, Vallejo, Stockton, or some place. Write and tell me about yourself.

Steve

I turn to my dad again and discover he has stopped grading papers and is watching me. "When were these letters written, Dad?"

"1968, '69"

"Where would a black man and a white girl go in 1969, especially in a small town like Vallejo or Stockton?"

"Where would they go today?"

Dear Aimai:

I do not know exactly what kind of answer you want, nor what intangible hopes you have for the future; so if this letter seems not to be the type of reply you want, I hope you realize that I wrote it to you as best as I can not knowing exactly what you had in mind. I write, hoping I will be the kind of person if not the exact kind you would like to have reply to your ad.

I love children and I love women. In general, I love being alive. Perhaps, then, it will be no great surprise to you that I am married, as this is the normal thing for one who loves life, women, and children. I will say more of my marriage in a little bit.

I am an engineer who graduated with honors from San Francisco State. At present, I am practicing my trade programming for an electronics firm and spend part of my time building sound equipment. I am twenty-seven. I like music, bowling, movies, and people.

In my first paragraph, I mentioned your intangible hopes. If one of these hopes is to be married, you would have to find someone who is marriageable. If your ad has been run in the hope of eventually finding a full-time father for your children, that is good. But

Alternative #1: If finding a full-time father is your immediate goal, I know I can never fulfill your needs and your children's needs, as I could not be that father as I have my own children to raise.

However, Alternative #2, if finding a full-time father is your long-term goal, and what you wish now is for someone to fill in the gap for a few years until you find him, then perhaps I could be this person.

There is a third possibility, Alternative #3, which I will now present. Simultaneously, I will try to explain the relationship between my wife and myself which makes it possible for me to write this letter to you.

Sarah and I were married five years ago when I was still going to school. Since we were both young at the time, we did not realize how much each of us was going to change. We had many arguments, but we learned to talk with each other and remain in love. Let me explain further:

During the initial five years of arguments, I became most upset when I could no longer have sex with my wife during the period she was pregnant with our first child.

Being very frustrated at this time, I found a girl of my own age who was willing to be my mistress. I grew to love her a great deal although I could only visit her occasionally. Sarah never suspected what I was doing with my spare time. Perhaps for some marriages, this would have been the end.

After consideration, I decided to tell Sarah about the fact that I had a mistress. Almost a year of talks ensued and, in the end, martial success reigned for us. I continued to see my friend until, sometime later, she found someone who could spend more time with her.

At present both my wife and myself are interested in finding a married couple who like ourselves has discovered it is possible to love more than one person. However, we have found it very difficult to find a married couple that we both can admire that much, for if the wife is a nice person, the husband turns out to be "so-so." And if the husband is okay, the wife is a "rat-fink", etc. Thus, our progress has been poor with married couples.

So now, I would like to mention the third alternative:

Sarah and I could help you find a husband. We would naturally hope that you and your new husband would be interested in wife swapping and husband swapping. However, if neither of you cared to swap partners that would be your own business.

We know a person (male) who is 28 and is recently being divorced by his wife. This experience has caused him to grow up in many ways. Although the divorce was not wholly the fault of either person, the divorce was the result of immaturity by both husband and wife.

He is a mechanical engineer like myself and has just completed his work on a masters degree in mechanical engineering (after taking a leave of absence from work). He is basically a decent and down to earth person.

I will not mention this letter to him since I do not know if you will reply or not; I do not like to raise false hopes.

I do not know many things about you, but I feel that it took courage for you to run your ad. I know that I would love to meet you whether you wish me for the temporary companion or not. I admire your spirit, wishing you luck.

  Bill

"Was there an Aimai Cristen?" I asked my dad one day. "I mean is she a real person or did you just make her up?"

"She was real." His tone suggested he wanted me to go on and ask him more about her.

"Well what was she like?" I asked, using my hands to indicate he should keep talking and not depend on me to prompt him.

"Sort of a scatterbrain," he replied, "Like you were for a few years before you got your act together."

"Oh sure. A scatterbrain?" I twisted my face up as if I'd been sucking on a lemon. "But it says in the ad, she was twenty-four?"

Dad looked at me with those dark penetrating eyes of his. "Aimai may never have got her life organized. I barely knew her, but she came across as if she didn't have any real purpose. You need purpose as much as food and water to keep yourself going."

"If you barely knew her, then how come you've got all her letters?"

"Oh, that." Dad's eyelids fluttered, a sure sign he was hiding something.

"That," I persisted.

"There's a big story behind these letters."

"Try me."

"You got all week?"

I smoothed the letter in my hand and put it back unread on the stack. "Sure do. That's why I moved home. To be with you, to have long father-daughter talks, remember."

"I remember. Sometimes, though, I wish..."

"You wish I hadn't come home."

"No!" My dad sat bolt upright in his chair. His sincerity, the vehemence of that single "No!" was undeniable. For a moment, I felt guilty for having challenged him. But just for a moment. He's never really told me that he loves me. If he has, it's been under the cover of darkness, sneaking into my room after I'm asleep, checking on me each night before he goes to bed himself. All right, maybe it's me that has something wrong with her, who needs constant reassurance her father really loves her. No real harm in getting my father to say he loves me, over and over, is there?

"I never wished you hadn't come home! Not for one moment, sweetheart. I treasure every minute you've been with me. And I missed you so often when you were gone. No, I wish you and your

18

sisters could have been around at other times during my life. The exciting, crazy times. Like when I met Aimai Cristen."

"Be there? I was minus six when you met her."

"Lighten up, will you. Be there in spirit. Inside my head. Share my feelings. Maybe, you were there. You could have been the man across the street, the one we didn't see, who fell on a banana peel and slipped under a moving car. Just an innocent passer by who got reincarnated as my daughter. Maybe you were the rock and roll drummer who stepped on the patch cord and electrocuted himself."

"But Aimai Cristen," I said impatiently, "Are you going to tell me her story? How did you meet her? Who introduced you? What was going on in your life?"

That strange expression came over his face, the one he gets when he's inside his head. For a moment, I thought I'd lost him and then, whoops, he's back.

"I responded to this ad in the Freep, the Los Angeles Free Press." He quoted from memory, "'Young attractive girl, 24, searching for love, compassion, joy from a man who can provide financial security. Write Aimai Cristen, Box 5689.'

"I was living in L.A. then, yo-yoing up and down the Pacific Coast like most aerospace engineers. From L.A. to San Francisco and back again. The remarkable thing was that whatever city you were in—Burbank, Sunnyvale, or San Diego, Missiles and Space had a branch there. If you got laid off in one place, you just applied to another. At best, you'd miss a day's pay. At worst, you lived off unemployment for a few months. I hear it's pretty much the same today. But a life like that is O.K., sort of, when you're single.

"Say I actually wrote something, part of a diary, during that period. You want to read it?

"Sure. Glad to."

He looked away for an instant trying to conceal his feelings. I could tell he was pleased. I said, "Well, you read my stuff."

He looked puzzled. "Your stuff?"

"Remember, all those papers I did in school: 'My summer vacation,' 'What I like about second grade,' 'The Pineers'—I really thought 'pioneers' was spelled that way because they cut down pine trees to build their houses. Wait. Remember the long essay I did in junior high school about teenage suicides."

"Do I? You got so depressed thinking about those kids that had killed themselves. We began to get worried about you."

"About a year too soon."

"Or maybe we didn't get around to getting worried soon enough?"

We weren't talking any more, my father and I, just sitting, looking at each other. I don't know who I saw sitting in his chair, my dad as he is now with all his gray hair, or that younger Dad, the one with a beard and the ripped pants he wore when he worked around the house, or the Dad, my dad, who came home from work in a business suit and tie and put me on his shoulder and carried me around the house while he looked for Mom. I wonder what he sees when he looks at my chair. Which of the many Dinos?

We have a wall between us. Momentarily, we pushed it aside; we touched, however briefly. He didn't tell me the story of Aimai Cristen that night, but I knew that sooner or later he would get around to it.

4. The Apartment

The manager had told Phil he could expect to find girls sitting around the pool in the evenings, and so, when evening came and the lights went on in the courtyard, Phil cocked his ears listening for sounds from below. All was silent apart from the complex's Muzak, on continuously, which played "Barefoot in the Park," and something that might once have been "Lucy in the Sky with Diamonds."

He peeked out the window finally, turning his back on the empty apartment—empty apart from his rented bed, his stereo, and the endless rolling contours of the sprayed acoustic ceiling—only to see a deserted courtyard and the safety lights reflected from the surface of the still, green pool.

"I'm not going to stay here and be alone," Phil said, addressing no one in particular. Shutting the apartment door firmly behind him, he stepped out on the landing that ran along the three long sides of the deserted courtyard. He knocked first on the door to his right. "Yes," came a girl's voice.

"I'm your next-door neighbor."

"I'm busy right now," she said, "could you come back later?"

"Sure," he said diffidently, then added a confident "I'll be back," to the closed door.

Phil repeated the same procedure at the door to the left of his apartment. No one responded. He stood for a moment in the silence, listening. From below, he heard a man's voice call, "They're not in." Phil walked to the edge of the landing and looked down to see the manager of the apartment complex looking up at him. "What are you doing?" the manager demanded.

"I'm just checking with my neighbor," Phil replied.

"Well, they're not in," the man said and stood, hands in his pockets, waiting for Phil to go back inside his own apartment.

"It's a quiet evening," Phil said conversationally.

The manager was unresponsive. "People are trying to eat their supper," he replied as if to suggest he would be inside eating his supper if he did not have to be on guard duty policing Phil.

"Thank you," Phil said, feeling that perhaps a thank-you was expected.

The manager glared, his face bright red in the reflections from the pool light. "Well," he said after a pause, "Aren't you going in?"

"Uh, yes, yes." Phil scurried inside his apartment and waited just inside the entranceway until he heard the manager's door close below. Then, he walked outside again, and tiptoed down the length of the long motel landing. When he felt he was out of earshot of the manager, he knocked on an apartment door.

"Yes?" A man came to the door, bare-chested, carrying a can of beer. He stood blocking the doorway, the sweat shining on his muscular body. Phil could see past him to where a slim blond was setting plates on the table. She did not look up. "Yeah?" the man said again.

"I just moved in," Phil said. "I was trying to meet people in the building."

"What's he want honey?" Phil heard the blond girl call.

"Nothing." The man swiveled his head so he could talk to his wife (girlfriend?) but his muscular torso continued to block the open doorway. He turned back to Phil: "We're going to eat, O.K.?"

"Later," Phil said. The man shut the door.

Phil continued down the landing. Sometimes he knocked, sometimes he just waited expectantly outside a door as if trying to feel out the character of the people inside. Most weren't home. Some called through the closed door that they were too busy to talk or they didn't want anything.

One man with a bushy mustache opened his door just as Phil was about to knock. He pushed by Phil quickly with a "Hi" and a friendly nod, and clattered down the stairs. As the man passed the manager's door, it opened and the manager came out. "Hi Al," he said. "Hi Arnie," Al called as he disappeared from the courtyard.

Arnie the apartment manager remained outside. His head turned slowly in an arc around the courtyard as if searching for Phil hiding on the landing above. Phil shrank back in the shadows and held his breath. Then Arnie went back into his apartment.

A woman came to one of the doors, finally. Phil talked to her, making up what he was going to say as he went along. "I'd love for you to meet my husband," she said after a pause. The couple stood in their doorway chatting with him. "An awful lot of single girls do live here," they both acknowledged, though they didn't offer any suggestions. The man thought kind of a cute blond lived back in the direction from which Phil had come. When he said this, his wife, a brunette, gave him a long slow look. They didn't invite Phil inside.

At last, he risked crossing to the opposite side of the courtyard where he would be in full view of the manager's searching eyes. A small card table stood outside the manager's office with a deck of cards and three glasses sitting on it. Phil knew he did not have long to continue his quest before the manager reappeared.

"I'm new to the apartment," Phil told the tall angular brunette who answered his next knock. For a while, they talked through her partially closed door. She shut the door for an instant while she fumbled with the chain, but opened it again quickly to invite him in.

"I'm a nurse," she said, after she'd brought two cups of coffee and a slice of cake to the table.

"I work as a computer programmer."

"That must be interesting," she said.

"Oh, not really, though it's fun at first."

He studied the girl closely. She was not attractive, but her smile was warm and friendly. The friendliest person I've met in LA, he thought, the only person I've met really outside of work.

"Do you read your Bible?" she asked, unexpectedly.

"Uh, sometimes."

"I've got one right here. We can read together."

She got up and fetched a very large Bible to the table. Her hips, he saw were slim and unformed, their movement almost sexless, though she still carried the same warm smile that had first greeted him in the doorway. She can't have many friends either, he thought, but I bet she's nice if you get to know her. He started to undress her in his mind and to touch her small breasts.

"You don't believe in evolution, do you?" she asked.

24

"Yes, I do," he said, his mind still not entirely on the conversation.

"That's not what the Bible says."

"Some of the things, the Bible says, I believe and some I don't," Phil persisted.

"You've got to believe them all," she said firmly.

She's serious about all this, Phil thought. For a moment, he had a vision of himself in a long patriarchal beard, a Bible-bearing Christian with a thin, angular brunette wife trailed by three angular brunette daughters. . .

The diary entry ended abruptly in the middle of the page.

"That's it?" I said to my father, "That's all you wrote?" He nodded his head. "Well, you got the number of daughters right in your dream anyway. But I'm the only one who's angular."

"You're O.K." he said, his eyes sparkling, "You're more than O.K. This girl was drab. You've got personality."

"So," I persisted, "what finally happened between you and her?"

"Nothing. She followed me out on the landing as I was trying to slip away, still carrying that Bible—it must have weighed a ton. Made me promise I'd come back and read it with her some more."

"Well you got to touch her breast, anyway."

"Touch her breast? What makes you think that?"

"You wrote it in the story."

"No. I wrote, 'he *thought* about touching her breast.' I never even got to put an arm around her. She wasn't my type. The worst part is that while I'm saying goodbye to her or trying to, the manager and his wife are outside playing cards. And they watch me as I walk back to my apartment, all the way around the U. I'd planned to knock on the door of the girl who lived in the apartment next to me, the one who said come back in half an hour, but with the two of them listening downstairs, I just went back inside my apartment, turned on the stereo to drown out the Muzak, and went to bed. Eight-thirty in the evening."

" For three weeks afterward, I pretty much did nothing except go to work and sit in my living room staring at the swimming pool. That's why I replied to Aimai Cristen's ad: sitting alone in that apartment at night like to drove me crazy."

5. The Appointment

The initial phone call from Aimai Cristen was interrupted. He could hear the slap, then the sound of a woman crying, and then someone hung up her telephone.

She phoned back the next evening at about the same time. She didn't mention the slap or the crying, but she did apologize for having to break off the call. Then she said she would like to meet him.

He began to describe how she could get to his place up in Chatsworth—he was new to the Southern California area then and had little or no idea how to get around himself, but she said no, she didn't have a car. "I'll drive down to see you," he said; "this evening?" he asked hesitantly.

"No, tomorrow night." They settled on the steps of the Santa Monica Public Library, the next evening at eight. From there, they would walk and talk, and then they'd see.

By the next night, he'd had plenty of time to worry. While he was out seeing Aimai Cristen, what was to prevent her and her accomplices from coming to his apartment and robbing him? For once he was grateful that the concierge, Arnie the apartment manager, lived in the apartment below. "Arnie," my dad said, "I'm going out this evening. I have a date with this girl I met through a want ad. Could you keep an eye on my apartment? And on me if I don't come back."

"I think you're crazy," Arnie said, "Going out with a girl you don't know."

Inwardly, my dad had to admit he probably was a little crazy. What sort of girl would you meet through a want ad?

Eight the next evening coincided with the library's closing. By the time Rafer arrived at the library—he'd missed the freeway exit and had to circle back through traffic—the library steps were deserted except for a crying girl who sat with her head bent forward and touching her knees. The girl's arms were wrapped around her legs as if she wanted to seal out everyone and everything around her.

"Are you Aimai Cristen?" he asked. The girl released a long anguished sob. Rafe was torn between a desire to help and the need to contact Aimai as soon as possible to see why they had missed connections if, indeed, they had missed them. "Can I help you?" he asked. The girl sobbed again.

Rafe sat down on the steps beside the crying girl. There was no doubt in his mind now that he'd missed his appointment. Damm, he should have left the apartment earlier. He shouldn't have taken the time to talk with Arnie. "What seems to be the trouble?" he inquired a second time.

The young girl both attracted and repelled him. Her long blond hair, bleached almost to the color of straw, was matted and unwashed. A deep, full tan that also pointed to many hours on the beach was hidden under layers of dirt. She was short, almost fragile with slender hands and wrists. Her bosoms barely broke the surface of her blouse.

"You never had a sister, did you?" his friend Pete had asked him once. He could not remember why Pete had asked him that. "Are you Aimai Cristen?" he asked.

The girl nodded her head; she could have been nodding "yes." Rafe loaned her his handkerchief and she used it to wipe away the tears and to blow her nose with a faint honking sound. She stopped crying and said she was glad to see him. "What's your sign?" she asked him, and "Do you like the beach?" She didn't seem to pay much attention to his answers.

After awhile, she began to talk about herself. Her words, welling up from somewhere deep inside her, were not really directed at him.

Her story was confusing. There were or had been parents. They didn't understand her. They'd died, one after the other, still not understanding,

28

though now she understood them and what they'd wanted for her. She wished she still had a chance to talk with them. She'd had a boy friend that was mean and, perhaps, she'd even had a baby. (She was very unclear about this. Did the baby live with her now? Had she given it up for adoption? Rafe didn't feel he knew her well enough to ask.) She'd even done some nude dancing. ("Professionally," he asked. "You'd better believe it honey.") And she had a boy friend or a brother who was constantly on and off drugs.

Rafe didn't know whether to laugh or to cry over what she was saying. Partly because the girl's words seemed so completely out of tune with their meaning. She would smile as she recalled the most gruesome of memories and, then, break into tears for no particular reason. He sat closer to her because he thought that was she wanted and put an arm around her shoulders. Not too close, because she did have an intense body odor. She needed a shower badly.

"Do you want to walk?" he asked hesitantly.

"Sure," she replied, "Or would you like to come to my place?" She had a place? Why didn't she wash then, clean herself, take a bath? "Sure," he replied, but already her thoughts seemed to have moved on to something else.

"My old man... my brother," she corrected herself, "he may be in jail."

"What!" For an instant, he was outraged. He'd never known anyone who'd been in jail, for more than a few hours anyway. "Part of a demonstration?"

She looked at him strangely. "Yeah. I haven't seen him in three days." She smiled, laughed, cried, then tried to smile again. She had a way of stroking her smile with her fingertips up and away from her mouth that was quite sexy and a way of pinching her nose with her fingers that was not. Finally, the smile got the better of the tears. "He steals; he shoplifts. To get money for us. They may have caught him."

"That's what generally happens when you steal." Rafe replied cruelly.

"Yeah. Bummer. That's what I told him. I was supposed to get a job, but then I got sick." She began to cry again. This time she pressed her face against Rafe's shoulder and burrowed her small body against him. He could feel her breasts, naked underneath her blouse, and found himself aroused despite his desire to keep her at a distance. She seemed to sense his reaction but did not pull away. "I should see if he's come back," she said from somewhere down at the level of Rafe's chest. She paused and looked up at Rafe. "If not, you could stay with me."

What I've written down here is based partly on what my father told me and partly on what I read in his diaries and, of course, on what I read in the fiction he's written or tried to write. With most of the events in his life that he's taken the time to write about, the different versions are more or less the same. Oh, sometimes in his fiction, my dad will give the characters names like Pete or Rafe, but they are really all he. But in the part that happens next, when he goes with Aimai Cristen to her apartment, the stories don't agree. I mean, even when he talked to me about it, he would sometimes give me one version of the story and sometimes another. I think he was ashamed and embarrassed—either because he'd had sex with Aimai Cristen or because he hadn't. So when I retell the story here, I've tried to indicate where I think he was telling the truth and where he was just making it up. But I can't be sure.

After driving up and down the beach roads of Venice for more than an hour without finding the girl's apartment, Rafe was finally willing to accept her admonition that you couldn't get there by car. Parking dangerously close to a small group of elderly teenagers who looked as if their sole means of support were stolen hubcaps and stereos, her apartment proved to be just one short half-block away. The one-way streets of Venice, the half lanes that required constant backtracking up and down the hills that led to the ocean, made feet the only reliable mode of transportation.

She knocked on the door of the small cottage. Nothing happened. She knocked a second time.

"My brother is not here," she said.

"Oh well," Rafe said, "We can always go for a drive or walk along the beach or something."

"You know," she said, "If we could get inside, I could show you all the letters I got in response to my ad, let you read them. We could sit and read the letters until my brother got back."

After looking gamely under the doormat and in an empty flowerpot for the key, and feeling over the archway, she announced, not unexpectedly, "the key's not here."

"Back door?" he queried.

"Maybe." Inspection of the back door was equally fruitless; besides, the path to the back door was overgrown with weeds and looked as if no one had ever hacked their way back there before. "Well?" she said.

"Well," he replied, accommodatingly.

"We could go through a window."

"Umm. Maybe that's not such a good idea. Why don't we just walk down to the beach?"

"Straight arrow," she accused.

I am turning into a straight arrow, he thought. And if her brother doesn't come back? (If it is her brother we're waiting for, and not her boyfriend.) He fantasized again about getting into the shower with the girl, about helping her wash. He thought about how she would look naked, the appearance of her slim body when she stepped out of the tub all brown and glowing, freshly clean for him. He could smell the way she would smell then or convinced himself he could. And he could feel the softness of her skin under his hands.

The girl rubbed her nose again, ending as always by pinching it between her thumb and her forefinger. He wished out loud she wouldn't do that. "You have such a pretty face. Why spoil it? Like a cat's face, no, a kitten's."

"I'd like to get inside the house before my brother gets back," she said. "You know, it would give us more time. To talk. To look at the letters."

31

She was toying now with the buttons on her blouse. He knew what she was doing or trying to do. But at least she was paying attention to him for a change.

"Do you think all the windows are locked?" he asked.

They tried the windows; all the ones at ground level proved to be locked. The only remaining window, which she said led into the bathroom, could be reached, but barely, if she stood on his shoulders.

He knelt down in a gymnast's position, while she put first one tiny foot and then another into each of his palms. She was close enough to his face then that she brushed his nose with a button on her blouse. She pushed down hard on the top of his head as he stood upright. Then she took a step upwards until she stood on his shoulders.

He could hear fumbling with the window, then a grating sound as she slid it to the side. She pressed down hard on his shoulders as she pushed herself upward one foot at a time. He looked up in time to catch a shoe on the bridge of his nose as she wedged herself through the narrow opening. In a moment, she called to him from the front door. "Over here," she said.

Up to this point in his story, Dad's various versions of the meeting have been pretty much all the same, at least I haven't been able to catch him in any obvious contradictions. But now there are three different versions, one I found in a half-finished story he'd written which I think he made up, one he told me the first time I asked, and one I'm just guessing at by fitting all the pieces together.

The big questions are, 1) How did they get into the house? (I think my father broke in.) 2) Did he have sex with Aimai? (I don't know.) 3) How did he get hold of the letters she'd received? (I think he stole them. I think when the brother came back, my Dad figured out it wasn't her brother at all but her lover or her old man as they called significant others back then. Probably, once the brother came back, Aimai ignored my Dad. My Dad got angry—he gets angry easily—and just walked out the door with the letters, figuring that way he would show her.)

The way my dad tells the story, he boosted Aimai in through the window (though another time, he said, "we had to smash the glass,"); they sat around and talked for a while and looked at the letters, then Aimai got a phone call. She told my dad it was from her brother and that he'd broken down somewhere on the highway and that she had to go get him. My dad offered to drive her but she said not to bother, she had her brother's car. ("I thought you said she said she didn't have a car?" I asked my dad once. "That's what she told me on the phone.") By way of apology, she told my dad he could have the letters. "She told me she was moving up to the Bay area with her brother and the letters wouldn't be any good to her anyway."

"Did you get her new address?" I asked my dad.

"I thought I had," he said.

Now, that's the way my dad told me the story. The way he wrote it is like this:

The living room of the apartment held an immense and eclectic collection of books, mainly hardcovers, almost all new and unopened. They were piled—there is no better word—on brick and board shelves that climbed almost to the ceiling. Rafe prowled the edges of the room, picking up and putting down books at random—the majority had never been opened before—while the girl fussed in the bathroom.

He heard the toilet flushing and the water running in the sink, but the girl was disheveled as ever when she reemerged. A rubber tube had been wrapped around her right arm and she held a hypodermic needle in her left hand. "Can you help me with this?" she asked.

"No. I don't think so. No. Definitely no." He had a fixed aversion to hard drugs. No good came from messing with your mind even if the trip were good. And the heavy penalties that came when they caught you later were definitely bad.

The girl stood waving her arm helplessly, started to cry, then disappeared again into the bathroom. She was out a moment later. "You've got to help me with the needle."

"I don't do drugs. Do it yourself."

"I don't know how."

"Well good; then you won't have any trouble breaking the habit."

"My old man, I mean, my brother always does it for me."

"I'm not your brother," Rafe said, exasperated. He and the girl stood toe to toe. Just far enough apart to trade blows. Or kisses. She's cute, he thought, but wow is she weird.

"Don't you like me?" she asked. She unbuttoned the remaining three buttons on her blouse. Her breasts were large and out of proportion to her emaciated body. But they bore stretch marks and were a sallow white color in contrast to the dark tan of her face and shoulders.

"Where are the letters?" he asked. "I've been wondering what the other guys wrote you. You said you got—how many letters—five hundred. Seems like a lot." I'm babbling, he thought.

"I know what you want," she said; she cupped one hand under her left breast and held it out toward him. The breast was white and puffy, its nipple small and almost invisible. Rafe reached out a hand, touched it.

"Uh, oh," said a slick black voice behind him, "Mustn't touch the merchandise."

Rafe looked up. The dude in the doorway might have modeled for all the "Pimp wanted" ads. He had the hat, the boots, even a cape around his shoulders.

"Don't turn around," the pimp warned. The slim brown hand poised familiarly on Rafe's shoulder made Rafe angry. He turned and struck out at the man but got only a fist in his nose and a bloody lip for his pains.

Rafe backed away, stumbling over the girl, and assumed a boxer's stance, left hand out and ready to jab, right hand cocked and waiting. The pimp laughed and threw another punch, a left. Rafe slipped inside it and began to hit the man with a flurry of lefts and rights.

"You shit," the girl said. He heard the floorboards creak, then everything went black and silent . . . .

When Rafe woke up, it could have been an hour or a minute later. Probably an hour. All the lights were on in the house. The piles of books were scattered around the room, and a half open box sat next to him. A note was pinned to it: "Try and find me, you shit." The letters, five hundred of them as promised, were in the box.

6. The Yo-Yo

It wouldn't really have mattered if Aimai Cristen had wanted to see my dad again or he had wanted to look for her. The next day my dad lost his job, no, he was fired.

I don't know the circumstances; my dad didn't give me the details. But losing a job was small potatoes in those days, my dad told me: "The demand for engineers and scientists far exceeded the supply and if the Missiles and Space in Burbank laid you off, then you just applied to the Missiles and Space plant up in San Jose."

So he said goodbye to Los Angeles—he really never was happy there—surrendered his deposit on the apartment, though not without a fuss, packed his pillows and bedding in the back of the car—"They were about all I owned except for a clock radio."—and drove north to San Francisco.

Back to Missiles and Space

The set might have been taken from Patrick McGooan's "The Prisoner," down to the heavy wire gate much higher than a man that slammed behind you on the way in. Guards inspected you and your belongings as you went in and out. Strangely, I always felt uneasier about the getting out than the getting in. The slam of the gate was just too final as it shut behind me in the mornings. And Patrick McGoohan's own adventures as #6 of the Village were just too close to my own work life for comfort.

The enormous bullpen we worked in was filled with 12 long rows of desks facing each other in pairs; one man sat with his back to the inner corridor, a second man was at the desk across from him, a third and fourth man sat at the desks on either side. And up against the walls of the enormous room were banks of secretaries and filing cabinets.

My specialty—even in those early days before my awakening—was giving back rubs to my coworkers. They might not have wanted them but they needed them. A lot of tension resided in that place, partly because we worked in such close proximity, partly because we were always under pressure to get the next contract, mostly because we were forced to live a series of lies.

Irv, my boss, would ask me how long it would take Nick and I to complete our portion of the program. I didn't have to ask Nick to know we were running about a month behind. "It could be two months," I'd tell Irv, "if Jim doesn't get back to us on Tuesday when he told me he would."

The memo from Irv to his boss, Don Coombs said "We hope to be able to complete the project within a week or so of the target date."

Copies of the memos from Don Coombs to his boss, the division manager, were circulated to everyone in the group. Regardless of what Irv wrote and confided to him in their weekly meetings, the memo from Coombs would read, "On target" and would be followed a week later by a memo from the division manger to the V.P. that said we were ahead of schedule. It was scary.

My specialty was tank warfare in Western Germany in some hypothetical World War III. I figured the Soviets for sure winners unless they were as messed up as we were.

The back rubs brought me two interesting contacts. The first was an older woman, a secretary, who asked me if I'd like to give a talk to a group of Boy Scout mothers. The second was a tall girl about my own age who told me I should look up the Free University.

Boy Scouts

What would I say to a group of Boy Scout mothers? I had decided, perhaps with an unjustified faith in my own ability as a lecturer, that I would wing it, perhaps putting together a talk as I listened to what the other speakers had to say.

For some reason, Mrs. Chalmers, the older woman in her forties who served as secretary for my group, seemed to think I could speak for the rebellious generation of 18- to 23-year olds who were then flocking to San Francisco. Not hardly. I was almost 30, well 28. And I didn't hang out, I worked 9 to 5 as an engineer.

But I did know what it was like to feel oppressed, unloved, and misunderstood. My own adolescence had been spent, like those of most other people I knew, on doing the exact opposite of what I really wanted. I went around with a chip on my shoulder, isolating myself, full of cold prickles instead of warm fuzzies, telling people I didn't care, when what I wanted most was a big warm hug.

Although the other speakers on the panel could not have been more than one or two years older than I was, I found himself receding further and further from their well-meant comments, the way I might have fled in adolescence from an aunt or uncle who was trying to understand me.

While they pontificated, I sat off by myself—I'd deliberately moved my chair to one side of the others—and thought, "nobody loves me, nobody cares what becomes of me, I hate them all," chanting it over and over again in my mind like a mantra. I let the chant take over my body; when the other speakers' words threatened to intrude on my feelings, I sent out waves of rage and isolation, pushing them back, back.

All my imagination? Well, you'll hear what happened.

Mine was the last talk on the program. By the time the other speakers had finished, I was almost inarticulate with rage and self-pity. "Our next speaker is Dr. Phillip Good," I heard Mrs. Chalmers say.

I didn't move from my chair.

"Dr. Good, Dr. Good? Are you all right?"

Don't you understand, I thought, trying to beam the signal from my brain to hers, I just want somebody to love me, somebody who will care for me.

"He's got stage fright," I heard someone whisper.

"That's all right, Dr. Good. If you're nervous, you don't have to speak." Mrs. Chalmers smiled sympathetically, as if to say I have children of my own, I understand how difficult adolescence can be.

I got up on my feet. Swayed. I wanted to scream, but my voice was little more than a croak. "I just want a hug," I heard myself say, finally.

Suddenly, a procession of women including Mrs. Chalmers and one or two of the other speakers were coming out of the audience and up on the stage to hug me.

"I was magnificent," my father said with that mixture of smugness and little-boy shyness that always makes me want to both hug him and kick him. He was partially right, but I wasn't ready to compliment him yet.

"Wait a minute, Dad. Was your anxiety real or was it just an act?"

"Well, at a certain point..." he began and paused.

"It got real," I finished for him. I thought about what he'd said. "You were right about adolescents wanting a hug, but your knowledge didn't help you and mom to understand me any better."

He reached out and touched my arm lightly with his fingers. I pulled away but only so I could take his hand in mine. We held hands, squeezed, looked away from each other.

(I don't know why Dana complains Dad's not easy to talk to. He's really easy to get along with. And I will talk to him about my problems soon.)

"How did you learn to do that?" I asked him, "To make yourself over into almost another person?"

He almost leaped in the air, immensely pleased by my understanding, overjoyed he was being understood. "It's peculiar you ask me that. You see, that day, I just did it. I only learned *how* to do it later."

The Free University

Although the second contact with the girl who said I should look up the Free University was even briefer than the first, it was to have a far greater and lasting influence on my life.

I found out where the girl lived, and when I did not run into her again at the office, I went to her house after work three or four days in a row and waited outside, hoping I would run into her.

40

When she answered the door, finally, she told me she'd been on vacation. She didn't invite me in. (Was somebody else, another man, inside?) But she did give me the address of the Free U.

I went over there immediately. (Impulse ruled my life when I was single. I'd go to work unhappy and then be overjoyed if I found ways to occupy myself after work until it was time to go to bed.)

The first question they asked me at the Free University was what I wanted to teach. "I don't know anything about it," I said.

"What better way to learn," countered the slender, stoop-shouldered man with a day's growth of beard who had posed the question. Everyone else in the Free U office had been dashing around madly when I walked in, sorting papers or talking on the telephone, and had either not looked up or had simply walked away when I tried to talk with them. Only this man was willing to meet my eye, this man and one somewhat overweight lady who told me she'd just heard about the Free U herself and wished that someone would give her some help.

The slender man said to me, "You'd really better make a decision what you're going to teach. The new catalog goes out this week."

"I really just wanted to meet people," I confessed.

"What better way than by teaching a course? You'll meet people who share your interests. No? What course will you teach?"

"The Kennedy Assassination," I said.

"Excellent!" he replied, his long, thin face radiating his pleasure. "What time of day?"

"Tuesday and Thursday from 5 to 6. Right after work." A funny sort of school, I thought, where you could make your own schedule.

"And where will you give the course?"

"Why here, I suppose. Do you have classrooms?"

"All the world is our classroom," the man said to me, "But we've none here, I'm afraid."

By now, I was passing quickly from puzzled to indignant, "We'll meet in the town square in Los Gatos, Tuesday and Thursday from 5 to 6," I muttered through clenched teeth.

"Excellent. Though it may be a little bit difficult for many of our students to get to you. Most of them live near here. But I'm sure you'll get a few. We'll have the course description in our next catalog."

"But," I said and paused, stymied. My only opportunity to develop a real life seemed to be rapidly fading away, "Is there any way I could attend any of the classes that are going on now?" I was almost begging.

"Well, I'm giving a class tonight," the man said.

"Just tell me how to get there." I took down the directions, made a copy—I got lost easily in those days—and then went off to kill time before the start of the class.

7. Free University Catalog I

Victrology

Interpretive Psychedelic Dancing (Miss Moore, the instructor, is a -
   working professional topless dancer)

Candlemaking

Winemaking

Breadmaking

Singing Around a Piano

The Wonderful World of Arts and Crafts. Instr: Sarah McCarthy

   If you want to be a serious artist or craftsman, this is not the
place for you. This class is for those who want to learn to enjoy
artwork. You do not have to worry about my approval. This is for
fun. We will do clay modeling, paper work, coloring, painting, group
painting, finger painting, and other things. Instructor is 8 years old.
Course will meet just once. Sunday, April 27th, 2:00 pm.

The Way Things Work. Instructor: Dan Ingalls

The aim of this course is to build the courage and technique needed to find out how things work and to fix them when they don't.

Me, Kathy Kirby

The Natural History of Fishes

Self Defense. Instructor: Ace Hayes

A course dealing with general situations in which one may need such skills

Amateur Night Psychodrama

8. Amateur Psychodrama—Tues 8PM—Robb Crist

Quaker that I be, I arrived early at the private home in a rural suburb near Stanford where the class was to be held. Was I the instructor, I was asked. No. All I knew about psychodrama was what I'd read in a book. Did this question from a complete stranger mean the instructor was not there yet? I was led out to the tree-walled garden by my hostess and stood where I was placed, idly running my hands over the bars of a children's play set. Five or six other people were already waiting there, and like me, they all seemed to be waiting for someone else. How to pass the time? Swing on the swing? I was a little large.

Others arrived: Friends of the hostess? of her children? Fat ladies in their mid-forties, one at a time until there were five of them on the bench in the garden. Our instructor-- forty minutes late--appeared briefly, then disappeared into the house with his disciples before returning to wander by himself through the garden. He was the same man who'd signed me up at the Free U that afternoon and talked me into teaching a course. I recognized him and waved, but he did not meet my eye.

From time to time, he stopped to chat individually with one or the other person in the garden. After a pause, I saw him stoop down to the ground beneath a tall oak tree. When he stood up, he was carrying something in his hand.

Were we ready to begin? Not quite. Our instructor had found a baby bird that had fallen from its nest in the oak tree. I knew of three different things one might do for a baby bird that has been separated from its mother:

return it to the spot where it fell or was kicked from the nest,

kill it at once and end its suffering,

spend the night and perhaps the next day masticating insects and transferring them beak to beak into the baby's mouth.

But there is a fourth foolish alternative, I hadn't conceived of: Discuss the bird at length, pass it from hand to hand, solicit opinions from one and all, until, when a vote is finally taken to resolve the conflict between the nice-fat-wormers and the bread-crumbs-in-warm-milks, the poor animal dies. With its final plaintive "cheap," the psychodrama can begin.

My own view, which it appeared I held alone, was that we should return the bird to the spot on the ground from which it had been removed. The response from the crowd was to attack me--not my opinions, but me. Or, perhaps, not me, for the proffered insights into my character bore little relation to my own opinion of myself. **(Oh Dad, I'm not surprised.)** For the most part, I judged them opinions that had been prerecorded, to be played back at a later time before a live audience.

The class was a bummer and I was ready to leave. I asked the instructor—"call me Robb"—Robb, then, whether this so-called psychodrama was to consist of a bunch of people ratfinking on one of their own number. That's not a psychodrama, I said, feelingly. "Take charge then," Robb said.

46

"Me?" Robb seemed as serious as he'd been that afternoon when he proposed I teach a course. (And how serious was that?) The idea was tempting. I thought back to what I remembered of my readings. "You take the part of your wife," I asked one man who I'd overheard earlier complaining about his spouse. "What's your name?"

"Art."

"And you be Art," I said to another, a broad-shouldered individual with just the beginnings of a potbelly. As if they'd been waiting the past ninety minutes for the opportunity to do just that, the two men proceeded to reenact a scene from that morning's breakfast table, just the way psychodrama is done in the text books. I relaxed, but too soon, I'm afraid. Verbal abuse became slaps. They woke the children. "You be a child," I said to a relatively young man with wisp of a moustache who'd been watching the scene intently. I had something in mind on the order of a sixteen-year old, but he began to goo and crawl toward his mother for milk. Then a second gooer joined in. The parents fondled their children and began to make up their quarrel. Not precisely what I had in mind.

(I put down the diary for a moment. Poor Dad, I thought. You really do need to have control.)

Two men and a girl sitting in a nearby corner seemed as bored as I. I suggested (brilliantly, I thought) that one of the males play the son of the other two. He was to pretend that he'd just come home and found his parents smoking pot (get it?). The girl looked through me as if I were a horse's ass. "You're a horse's ass," she said, "That's not real, that's not Chung."

"We must learn to cope with unreality," I replied, using one of my better pre-recorded lines. She looked past me, unresponsive.

On the floor, the original gooer had broken into screams, as if there were an all-too real pin in his imaginary diaper. Someone put on a record, raised the volume louder and louder until it drowned out the baby's cries. A father-image strode across the living-room floor and turned down the record player. Someone turned it up again.

"Turn it down," the father-image demanded.

"No. Let him be," cried a young man near me, "Playing records is his thing."

"Yelling orders is my thing."

One boy/man shoved another. One boy/man shoved back. They wrestled on the floor.

"Stop," someone called. They stopped. Two held the one on the floor. "Go," hollered the same voice, Robb's voice. I looked across the room and saw that Robb had taken control. The boy/man on the floor squirmed, lifted an arm, kicked. "Stop," Robb called. They stopped. Four men held the boy/man on the floor. "Go." The boy screamed, "mother-fucker" and bit the man who'd been foolish enough to put his hand over the boy's mouth. The boy turned red till the veins stood out on his forehead, then white, as if he were going into shock. Rage, rage, rage!

The girl in the corner, the one in the granny gown complete with apron who'd rejected my wit a few moments before, hurtled through the air like a cat, claws outstretched, screaming "get him," as she went for the boy's testicles. Thankfully, Robb, who'd sat quiet and pensive,

48

almost uninvolved through the preceding struggle, batted her aside like a ping-pong ball, bare inches from her target. Trajectory interrupted, she landed on one of the four men who'd been holding the boy down. He crashed in turn against two other bystanders and began to scream obscenities. The girl could be heard crying, the boy raged, the man at the record player put on the Beetle's "Hard Days Night," and I tiptoed quietly and wisely from the room.

The evening air was fresh and cool. I could see the shadow of the coastal mountains in the moonlight. The instructor and two other men, including the one who had portrayed the husband who had beat his wife, approached me. "You can't leave now," they said.

"But I am leaving," I replied.

"But we're all together, like people on a ship. You can't leave until we return to port."

"Goodbye," I said. Was I the only one in Palo Alto who still went to work in the morning?

They watched as I walked away. Did I mention that all this had taken place far from town? At least five miles from a freeway exit, twenty minutes at freeway speeds, then five more miles along back country roads until I reached my own apartment? I supply this much detail only because as one of the first to arrive and park, I now found that thirty-five automobiles were parked three abreast behind my own.

Forward. A return to the house with the garden would be anticlimactic (and very embarrassing). I walked on. After perhaps fifty yards, the driveway exited on a dirt road. A car came toward me. I stuck out my thumb.

The diary entry ended here.

Has my father read his own diaries, I wonder. Many of the things about him that annoy me the most are revealed here in stark clarity in a diary written twenty years before:

he has a preconceived notion of how things must be done; it must always be done his way or not at all; he must always be in control; he is always right and, win or lose, other people are always wrong. Here, as always, he has run away from conflict instead of confronting it, but then, this is exactly my own problem or it used to be.

This diary entry also reveals many of the characteristics that make my father one of the most lovable of men: his willingness to try new things and to work through early failure, his refusal to be intimidated, his indifference to the opinions of others and, at the same time, his desire to do right by them. I wonder if he has ever reread these diaries. I think they would do him good.

"Dad, about your diaries?"

"Yes." (His voice is on a rising note, inquisitive, though his tone remains detached, the morning paper only an inch or two lower than when I first spoke.)

"You're sure it's all right if I read them?"

A nod accompanies a light rustling of the paper.

"I've been reading about the time you went to the encounter--the house in the woods, the dead bird in the garden. Do you remember?"

The paper comes down. "That was my first encounter. Of course, I remember."

I pause, thinking how I will phrase what I need to say: "Dad, there is something about the way you write. Your style."

"My style?"

"Oh, you have a very good style." I can see he is very concerned with my reaction to his writing. I will have to be very careful in choosing my words. "I mean, tremendous imagery. I can see what you are writing about almost as if I were there myself."

"Yes. Yes." He burbles with joy. "Joyce hurtling across the room. Martin and I wrestling on the floor."

"Well, yes. The activity is all there, Dad, but in a way, you're not there. Your writing is very detached."

"Like a fly on the wall."

"But you're not a fly, Dad. You're a human being and I don't have any real sense of what the encounter meant to you, of what was going on inside, of how you felt. Were you disturbed? angry ? resentful?"

He did not reply.

I wanted them all to like me. It's no easy thing wanting people to like you. Afraid they won't, you hold back, aloof, let others make the first move. Of course, not everyone will or can like you. But oh, I wanted them to like me so much. I was so afraid they wouldn't. I can't tell my daughter about the fear

9. Free University Catalog II

The Kennedy Assassination—Was it really a CIA plot to put one of - their own, George Bush, in charge of the country?--Los Gatos town square, TT 5-6—Phillip Good, Ph.D.

Care and Feeding of Sailboats

Turning on Social Systems   Dr Joel Fort

Hypnosis

I Ching

Absurd Theatrical Happenings—Don't be a Jabberwock; take this - course.

Educate or Eviscerate?   Do we really need to pass on our cultural traditions?

Arc Welding Junk Sculpture   Sue

Meeting People -- a one-day event -- #6

52

Creating a People's School

Searching for the Dolphin

Out into That World: Are you a woman who is feeling frantic or - bored with the suburban game--considering divorce--perhaps separated--or not, but wondering if it is what you want, and what about the kids?

Is Your Guy Gay?

Dessert: Kathy Kirby and Larry Tessler. Are you unhappy? Is it - because you turn down happiness when it is offered to you, or because you are afraid of the consequences, or because you don't have room for happiness? Think about desserts. Do you turn them down? Limit yourself to just one? If so, this class will teach you happiness acceptance via dessert acceptance. Meets a) after the general meeting on Larry's birthday (do you celebrate yours?); b) under the full moon during the Festival of World Goodwill; and c) at the Summer Solstice. Desserts: a) birthday cake, b) strawberry shortcake and muscato amabile; c) watermelon surprise, butter orange floats and lichee nut cheesecake.

[Last time we checked--in the early ninties--Kathy was a chiropractor in Santa Monica, Larry was the VP of R&D with Apple Inc's Macintosh group, and Phillip Good, a.k.a. #6, was Calloway Professor of Computer Science at Fort Valley State College.]

10. The Weekly Barb

FUMP

The Mid-Peninsula Free University has a new coordinator. John Dolly was elected at the FUMP general meeting Sunday.

John, a Free-U member for only three months, was elected with little or no opposition.

John is living and working with Vic Lovell's psychodramatic commune.

John's election is a blessing in disguise for the debt-ridden Free University. John is single and will be getting $200 a month, a healthy drop from the $600 a month needed to support former co-coordinator Bob Collumbine and his family.

John hopes to relate FUMP more to Stanford activists: "I think it was sickening how little support the Free U gave the April 3rd Movement last year."

In other business, FUMP voted to raise its fees from ten to thirteen dollars.   —- #6

Gays Meet

What a tremendous discouragement to creativity this is — to be called upon to build one's joy with one's academic colleagues entirely out of ideas. " (Martin Langer)

A second All-Gay Symposium takes place at the Wesleyan Center, Dan and Bancroft Way, December 26-30. The 28th is reserved for the West Coast Gay Liberation Conference.

Intent of the symposium is to permit gay scientists, mathematicians, and engineers, gay poets and artists to discuss their work.

There will be a poetry reading on Friday starting at 7 p.m. interspersed with lectures on the occult and religion. A program of songs written and sung by Rusty Eliot follows.

"I am an artist first, a homosexual second," Rusty says, "My songs deal with life, with love, and a little politics. They're not limited to sex."

The symposium will be climaxed by an unrehearsed play "What Has Come over Us" directed by the author.

"Rat-a-tat, tat"

Went the Drum

Come to People's Park.

Park Off

The University of California Regents opened the east end of People's Park to parking this morning. The Telegraph Liberation movement immediately

arranged to station pickets at either end of the lot. The pickets are asking, quite simply, that we do not park on our brother's grave. They have put up a sign on one of the parking stalls: Reserved for J. Rector.

Through a Fence Darkly

Florence Ragle, praised by the Establishment and dammed by the People for her one-woman crusade, parked again in People's Park last week, an insult to James Rector's memory.

At ten past ten in the morning before the picketers had arrived, the near octogenarian drove her old two-door Studebaker onto the lot and parked on the east side next to the parking-ticket machine. Her car stood alone in the midst of the gravel wasteland that had once been grass and flowers. There were no picketers and no other cars.

"Why are you parking here?" I asked her. She's been spat on, threatened and had her shirt damaged, but still she keeps on trucking. "Is it just a matter of convenience?"

"Not at all," she said. "I'm arthritic and it's a long (unnecessary) walk from here to the University library where I go each day to do my research.

"But this land that you call James Rector's grave belongs to the University. These people can't repeal the law of eminent domain."

How had this woman come by her opinions, I wondered. Was she a John Bircher? I talked to her for a half hour that morning and it blew my mind.

"I believe in socialized medicine," she said. "Linus Pauling and Dr Spock are my heroes. I'm a member of East Bay Women for Peace. (Women for Peace denounced Ragle's stance in a letter to the Gazette this week).

"I've not always been an activist," she said. "When I first started teaching years ago, I told the children about syphilis. I got in trouble for talking about a 'profane' disease. So I shut up."

"But you're speaking up now," I said.

"Yes," she said, "Somebody has to stop these bearded animals."

A second car drove into the lot and parked next to Florence's. Again the driver was a woman. I asked the new arrival about her politics.

"I just parked it," she said. "I parked my car here because there was no parking near Nicole's where I usually park."

Number Six

"So you really wrote for the Barb?"

"Uh-huh."

Now that I've finally been persuaded to move back home, my father spends more and more of his time with his head buried in the newspaper. Where is the vaunted togetherness, I was promised?

While he reads the paper, I browse through another of those water-stained boxes he drags around with him, seemingly forever. How many times did I help my Dad load and unload a moving truck with these self-same boxes? And what do the boxes contain? Mouse droppings, newspaper clippings, and half a dozen of those ubiquitous brown manila envelopes. In one of these, I found a series of articles clipped from the Berkeley Barb, circa 1969 to 1970.

Some had his name on them, some no byline at all, and some the cryptic "Number Six," or "6."

"Was that your pseudonym?" I asked.

"What's that?" Again the nose issued forth briefly from the paper; the spectacles were removed.

"Was 'Number Six' your pseudonym?"

"Yeah."

See what I mean? Great conversationalist my dad, great togetherness.

He's written some strange articles: "The Jollity Building," "Strawberry Creekwater Revival," "Eviction Notice," "Brothers Beware," "I Shared Love with a Topless Commune."

I began to read out loud, "'I shared an afternoon of love, joy, and compassion with a group of intimate caring people...'

Hmm. I wonder where he picked up that phrase 'love, joy, compassion?'

"Writer's prerogative," he snapped.

I continued reading,

I Shared Love with a Topless Commune

I talked with them about salaries and about dirty old men. I talked with some of the straight members about work and about fun. I watched the commune separate and join and grow.

I had learned about the commune while leafing through the Mid-Peninsula Free University catalog. A course for anxious homosexuals and a course in communal living met there.

A NOTE

Before coming over, I'd phoned for 'Ruth' or 'Rachel' in accordance with a note I'd found in the Free U nest. The note said that both of these girls could help me become a topless dancer.

The door was open. I stepped inside somewhat reluctant to intrude, yet feeling that the house itself was inviting me in.

I must have been right. I found two people, a boy and a girl, hard at work in the dining room. Neither looked up when I arrived. After a short interval, when the boy was getting up for another reason, he said, "Can I pour you a cup of coffee too?"

PEARS

Ruth came in then. I added my papers to those strewn on the tabletop and began interviewing. Ruth seemed somewhat mousy, a poor copy of her nude photograph on the wall opposite. She had small breasts and a pear-shaped rear hanging well down over her thighs.

Ruth has a B.A. in clinical psychology. She writes, speaks volumes on any subject, and paints. She's made 'the movies' (meaning nudies) and done volunteer work with the mentally retarded. It is she who is leading the Free-U course for homosexuals who want to get straight.

On the subject of topless dancing and wages she seemed somewhat confused. Her ad had promised $50 an evening in tips but she, herself, seldom made over $20. One could get $4 to $6 an hour depending. Depending on which and how many of one's hours one actually got paid for.

Each of the girls at the Ten Club has her own stage and her own customers who sit at adjoining tables.

CROTCH

"What I like to do," Ruth told me, "is sit on the stage apron showing off my crotch and play little games with my customers.

"You know? Like I'll pretend I'm trying to memorize their names. I'll have each one say his name out loud and then I'll try to say them back. The crowd enjoys laughing at my mistakes and that laughter sells beer.

"Not only that, but often I'll have them get up and trade places with each other at their tables; it turns into a regular encounter."

I told Ruth I felt she really liked these people —the straights and squares that patronized her club.

PRE-VERTS

"Hell, no," she replied, "they are nothing but a bunch of voyeurs and pre-verts."

By this time, the living room was crowded with the other members of the commune —Glenn, who is Ruth's old man, Larry, Mitzie, Rachel, and Suzanne.

Rachel is just twenty. She's five feet two, 100 pounds, brunette hair and brown-on-bottom, green-on-top eyes.

The cutest one in the house is buxom, eighteen year old Suzanne, but she doesn't dance. She's secretary to the boss at the Ten Club.

BEDROOM

The two young girls and I went to the small bedroom that they share at the back of the house.

Suzanne is from Alabama — Huntsville judging by the slight Yankee debasement of her Southern accent. She was seduced into communal living at a meeting of the Young Republicans: Rod the founder of their commune was conducting an economic seminar.

"We're both anarchists," Suzanne told me. "I dug what he was saying and I and about four other kids stayed behind after the seminar to hear more.

DISCOVERY

We were sitting together on Suzanne's bed, and Suzanne and I took the opportunity to explore one another while Rachel talked about her job at the Ten Club. A life-size nude poster of Rachel on the wall seemed to be doing the talking:

"I turned twenty on August the 12th and it took me two weeks to let myself accept that I would be working topless.

"But I like the job. I like talking to customers. I wouldn't want those old men to touch me — (authors' note —'old' to Rachel is 30 on up) —and I would have them thrown out if they did, though I would like to be touched by some of the kids, the young ones my own age."

Suzanne and I nodded, our heads touching.

"I dance. I like to dance. I like to sing too, from Sweet Judy Blue Eyes, especially where the song says 'It's hard.'"

NOT MUCH

Rachel watches daytime TV, but not much. She draws —but not much. She works leather and is learning to play the guitar — but not much. She does ball but very selectively. On her off nights, she drinks codeine, though she's found she has to space it.

"If I drink one bottle on top of another, like the next night there is nothing."

Five hours a night, four nights a week at the Ten Club. It's those times on stage, she says she comes totally alive.

"If anything pisses me, it's the way some customers scratch their crotches, rest their hands on their cocks, usually under their raincoats..."

I had Suzanne's panties down below her knees. I nuzzled her sweatshirt and she lifted it above her swollen nipples so that I could suck them directly. Her hands were as busy in my lap as my fingers were inside her tiny cunt.

RAPPER

Rachel kept rapping though I had long ceased to take notes:

"My job is to make the customers think they turn me on even if they really don't. One time though, there was this really young guy looking up at me from the edge of the stage. He said, "I'll do it to you all night long," and I did get turned on."

She paused as if allowing the memory to take over her body once again. "Good-bye now," she said and almost ran from the room.

Suzanne's cunt was tight and unyielding, tighter than that of any other woman I had known. Breath of pinewood, mist of sand-clay hollows. I burst inside her, fled small and lonely, gathered my clothes and walked back to the front of the house to complete my interviews.

HOLD THIS END

Ruth and her old man were tinkering with a weird-looking electrical apparatus: "Hold this end," they said, handing me a wire. I backed away, sensibly as it proved, judging by its effect on their ultimate victim. "It's for Ruth's class," Glenn said. "If they can steel themselves to withstand the electric shock, they'll be less afraid of hurt in a personal encounter.

"Did you get the interview?" he continued. I nodded. "Maybe you'd like to know something about our commune. We've been together about six months; we've got a regular work schedule — everybody has a task —it's posted on the refrigerator. We're organized if not together."

CRASHER

"There's the crasher problem," Ruth interjected.

"Yeah. I mean like some people in the house think we ought to put up everybody who comes along, some people say, "no, just friends," and some people think even that's an imposition on the house."

"You can get some bummers," Ruth said.

"Yeah, but you can get some good people. Eddy, that's Suzanne's friend from Alabama, he wants to study marine biology at Stanford."

"You know," Ruth said, "If you want to get this all down at once, come look at the list we drew up."

She pointed to a piece of yellow paper pinned to the bulletin board. On it were questions concerning crashers, ownership of property, sharing, pets, diet and drugs.

DECISIONS

For instance: Do you want a very clean pad or a "lived-in" house? What are you —personally — willing to do to keep up the yard and house?

"We aren't really together yet," Glenn said. "One of our problems is that we all work at different times. So we're trying to arrange to do at least one group thing a week even if it's only going to a movie.

"Last night, I held a non-verbal encounter for whomever was around and I'm going to repeat it next week."

Suzanne came back into the room; I smiled, but she sat down on the far end of the sofa away from me. Tom, the Britisher walked in too, but didn't say anything. He seemed angry. The atmosphere in the commune was beginning to get uptight, the hostility directed at me.

TRADE-OFFS?

One of the other questions on the list, question one in fact, was "Should people from within the commune trade sex partners? Should there also be sex partners from outside?"

"Maybe you had better tell me a bit more about your job at the club," I said to Ruth.

"Well, what's there to tell? We get bonuses, $20 a night, if we sell over a certain amount of beer. I haven't got a bonus lately — business has been bad because of all the raids on the club. There's another bonus of one hundred dollars each week for the girl who sells the most alcohol.

"I sell a lot of beer, of course. Like I said, it's a matter of working with the customers. I've got a lot of regulars.

DEPRIVED

"The guys who come once are either over 40 or under 20. If they're over 40, their wife has probably been undressing all this time in the closet and then she puts on her nightgown before she comes out. The Ten Club is the first chance they get to see pussy.

Same thing for the under twenty-
four year olds.

"The regulars as far as I'm
concerned are just abnormal and
perverted."

"Maybe they aren't getting it at
home," Rachel put in.

"There is something wrong with
all of them," Ruth went on
ignoring Rachel, "What kind of a
guy gets all his jollies in a night
club? If you ask me, they've got
nowhere else to go."

A SHIT

"Does your father...?" I began.

"My father is 53 and a head.
He's only worried that his little
daughter might get busted."

"My father is a shit," Rachel
screamed. "He's a doctor; he's
got six children and he made me
sell my daughter to pay for the
hospital bills."

She began to cry.

"Why don't you go," Tom said.
"We're a family."

I left the house at 4040 Olive but
I carried some very special
memories with me.

After I finished reading my father's article, I thought about it for a long time before saying anything. My dad has a great writing style, I think. Some of the things they worried about back in the sixties, like how to deal with crashers, ownership of property, sharing, pets, diet, and drugs are still problems today. But I had something else I wanted to talk about with him:

"Mist of pine hollow," I repeated, "very poetic. Did you really make love to that girl during the interview?" I asked casually.

"Yes," he snapped, and then looked up at me, embarrassed. He had remembered, suddenly, I think, that I was not merely an audience for his writings, but his daughter, and that something more of an explanation, perhaps even a mini-lecture might be called for. The longer the pause before he answered, the more difficult it became for him to say the right thing.

"You've got to realize," he said, "that this story was written at a different time, a different place; we did things differently in those days."

"You wouldn't advise me to behave the way the young girl, Suzanne, did?" I intoned, increasing the pressure.

"No!" he practically shouted.

"Well, is sex bad then?"

He shook his head, looked embarrassed. My dad, embarrassed?

"Well what kind of advice would you give a young person, say your daughter, today?"

He looked up at me for a moment to see if I was having him on. A series of expressions played across his face, shame, amusement, and then, something sterner. I could see he'd made a decision, decided even if I were having fun with him, even if he was embarrassed, that it was still his duty —whether I paid attention or not —to advise me what to do. I had the impression —I've seen how

72

my dad has behaved around women since I moved in with him —that he still wasn't sure about the guidelines himself.

"The first and most important rule is to respect yourself," he said.

"Respect yourself," I repeated slowly, drawing the words out in a parody of his professorial style. "I see. And is that what that little girl from Alabama was doing, the one who was sitting in your lap while you undressed her? I mean you'd just met."

My gibe didn't phase him. As always when my father and I have a discussion, he plowed on as if he hadn't heard my half of the conversation. "The next important rule is to be discrete. I told you that back when you started high school. You don't want to fool around, because you don't want to get a reputation."

"Was this girl from Alabama discrete? I mean having sex with a Barb reporter? Three hundred thousand subscribers reading in their morning paper how she'd had sex with him ten minutes after they'd met."

"I didn't use her real name."

"Just the fact that she was young, lived in a topless commune, whatever that is, worked in a topless bar as a secretary, and came from Alabama. I can see her parents back home in Huntsville or wherever getting a copy of your paper and saying, 'Oh my gosh, it's Sally.' How would you feel reading about me that way?"

This question seemed to give him pause. He screwed up his mouth as though he were sucking on a lemon before he said. "You know, it is very difficult to talk about sex with your daughter."

"Well, I'm glad you're finally doing it."

"Me too." He smiled.

"Did she really smell like a pine hollow?"

"Yes she did. Kind of cute. Short. Small-breasted. She was the cashier at the nightclub. You know, I never saw her again."

(Hey. Was something happening here? Was my dad talking to me like he and I were both human beings? Not professor to student or father to daughter, but genuinely sharing his feelings with someone he cared for.) "Did you want to?"

"Yes. I did. But I'd lost the phone number and was never able to find my way back to that house."

This sounded like my dad all right. I had a quick vision of him driving around in the near darkness in Menlo Park, cars whizzing by him on the left forced over to the wrong side of the street, as he slowly scanned house numbers trying to recognize the house he wanted.

"You wrote that the girl from Alabama was small breasted. Is that what you like?"

His mouth dropped open.

"Small breasts, like me." I said. I could not believe that I'd said it, not to my dad.

"You're, O.K. I mean...."

"Just O.K., O.K. or really great? I mean breasts are important. Look at Donna. She's always got boy friends. All she's got to do is stand there with her chest out and they walk up to her."

"Wait. Breasts are important. Not their size though. Their shape. But breasts are not everything. Donna is also a natural athlete. Does anything she wants to —soccer, volleyball, tennis, and gets it right the first time she tries it. She's not just big boobs."

I wasn't going to let him off the hook that easily. "And the thing about Dana, I suppose, is her brains?"

My dad leaned back, picked up a pencil as if he wanted to use it to illustrate some point, then put it down again.

"Actually, I always thought you were the brightest one in the family. You just never had the discipline. Dana has worked hard to get where she is. She admits it. The difference between you and Dana is the number of rewrites."

True, I thought, and changed the subject. "Dana, Donna, and Dina. How did you ever come up with those names?"

"It was your mother's idea. Or maybe it was both of ours. It started out as a joke just before you were born. Dana is a family name, some Aunt of your mother's. Donna was a compromise, the name of one of the nurses in the preemie ward; we used her name when your mom and I couldn't agree on anything else —I wanted Elizabeth Scott after a famous woman mathematician, but your mother wouldn't hear of it. We called you Dina for a joke when you were still in your mother's tummy."

"Her uterus."

"O.K. her uterus, I'm glad you're getting the terms correct.

"And you're changing the subject. Are you or aren't you a breast man?"

"No, you're changing the subject. What you're really asking me is how do I feel about your breasts. Isn't that what daughters are always asking their fathers, how do you feel about me as a woman. Well, when I married your mother, she looked just like you, O.K. Not like Dana or Donna. She only looks a little more like them now because she gained weight as she got older."

"And I suppose my breasts will get bigger like hers after I get pregnant."

"Yes they will. But don't get pregnant, yet."

"I'm not planning to."

"Good."

"This month." I couldn't help adding

"Thanks." He grinned.

I looked at him. He looked at me. It's strange how for such a voluble family, so much of our communication is done through glances or presses with the hand and fingertips. His look, I think, says I love you Dina. And I know the look I give him in return says, I love you Dad.

Garrison Grins

Edgar Labat and Clifton Alton Poret were free last week after spending over fourteen years on death row.

The two blacks, now in their forties, were sentenced by an all-white jury to die for the 1950 rape of a white woman.

In April 1967, the Supreme Court reversed their convictions. But for two and a half additional years, the two lived in the shadow off death because of New Orleans District Attorney Jim 'Jolly Green' Garrison's inattention to their case.

BARB asked Dr Phillip Good, a Bay Area statistician who worked on the Negroes' case, how he felt about the prisoners' release. Dr. Good had prepared the analysis of

racial discrimination in jury
selection used by the Court
in making its determination.
"They're just getting out
now!" Good exclaimed and
added ...

"Wait a minute. You interviewed yourself, Dad?"

"Sure. Did it all the time when I wrote for the Barb. Whenever I needed an expert on something or other. That way, I always got the quotes right."

I shook my head. Somehow, I'd always thought of the two parts of my father —the scientist and the underground reporter —as separate. Now, the two were coming together in my mind. He was less of an academic and more of a human being. Wasn't that what I'd always wanted?

"Dad?" I waited till I had his attention, "What if I'd made a mistake?"

He didn't say anything, which didn't make it any easier for me to tell him, "with boys, I mean?" He was there for me, I could tell, but still he didn't say anything. I wanted more. God, how did I know what I wanted? I wanted him to know without being told, to understand, to encourage. I wanted him to see me as I am and like me. "What will I tell other boys?"

"Nothing."

"But suppose they already know?" My face was flushed. I was grinning, but the grin was eating away at my face. And I was finding it harder and harder to smile. I wanted but was afraid to cry.

My dad put his arms around me and hugged me.

(Thank you, thank you, thank you, Dad.)

"Where are you?" he said

"I'm here with you."

"When is it?"

"When?"

"When."

"Now."

"Here and now, you are the brightest and prettiest of my daughters, the best partner that any man could ever ask for."

"Really?" I was smiling, I was crying.

"Really."

11. Tripping

I got a letter from my great aunt, today. After I found my Dad's stuff in the garage, I started writing to all my relatives. You see, I am trying to find out who I am.

> What's so special about the sixties, you ask me? It was just
> a great time to be alive. We all had jobs. We all thought
> that anything was possible. I was married, of course. Leon
> was alive. It was a good time. Boy do I miss him.
>
> Val

Dear Phillip:

Thanks for your letter. Programming at
Missiles and Space has its ups and downs. The
bank extensions I'm doing are behind schedule,
but my priority-ranking program seems to be on
the verge of working. I hear rumors of a 30%
layoff in March. Wonder what's true...?

Charlie

Dear Pig:

On Wednesday, February 26, I cleaned off my desktop,
carefully locked the desk, straightened out the
bookcase and generally made my M&S office neat and
tidy. Then I walked out. I have not been back and I
don't intend to go back.

I spent four days in the Santa Cruz mountains and
at Pescadaro beach. I had my dog with me and except
for him, I was alone. I had a feeling of freedom that I
had not experienced in years. I even smiled every now
and then.

On Monday, I walked into the office of an old friend
of mine and asked for a job. He put me right to work
and within the hour I was in a staff meeting.

I am working in M&S Building 32 at the La Loma
facility and my job is to generate requirements for the
programming group.

My desk is in a room with three others. I am not a
manager, I have no secretary. I have to keep up my
time card like an ordinary mortal and I am relaxed.

I had been a manager at M&S for over seven years
and had been the whole route. I have no regrets.

I have no idea of what the future holds. I don't know if the new job will work out (it's not really my line of work) but I did preserve a modicum of self-respect.

Good luck with all your enterprises in the city of brotherly love (hah).

Bill

12. Sister

I have another sister.

I found her picture at the bottom of one of the boxes. She can't be more than three or four months old. On the back of the photograph it says, "Katherine Good, January 1962." Katherine is my mother's name, but this is someone else. This Katherine looks like my dad or maybe like me —like my baby pictures, that is. Perhaps, she looks more like Dana when she was a baby, though Katherine's face is fatter than Dana's and her hair is darker.

Why didn't Dad tell us we had another sister? Or, are there two of them? I found a second photo. It's a Polaroid of the sort they take in hospitals. This time the child, another girl, can't be more than a few hours old, days at most. Amelia is the name on the back of the photograph, along with the date in late 1968. Again there is the strong family resemblance. You can see the same eyes, the same cheekbones in moo grandma —she's my dad's mother, and in my dad's grandfather —moo grandma's dad, as you see in my dad and in me. I should ask Dad about the two photographs, my two new sisters, but I probably won't. Maybe I will find something about them in the letters.

Dear Phillip

Well, Aimai and little Amelia are now in San Francisco, somewhere in the Haight. I'm not supposed to tell you the address. Clarence, that's the guy Aimai is living with, is really very nice although you probably wouldn't like him.

Your story of your final meeting with Carole sounds like something out of a horror film.

I can still imagine the scene in her lawyer's office:

You, Carole—larger than life, as you always spoke of her, her attorney, her new husband, and your child, all in one small room not much larger than the table around which you were sitting. Did you have someone with you for support?

You're eyes are focused on the child you hadn't seen in eight years, searching for some detail that will tie her irretrievably to you. You wrote you were too moved to speak. Or were you—and I hope this was the reason—remaining silent so that your daughter would adjust to your presence and have a chance to overcome her own very real fears?

Silence. No one speaking, the tension building in the room, and then your ex-wife, face red, cheeks puffed out, hollering, "Well, visit. You said you wanted to visit with your child. Now visit!"

Phillip, think of this, you were probably not the only one in that room who felt uncomfortable with her anger. I can imagine—and Phillip you will forgive me for writing this—I do love you in my own twisted Rosemary way—that under pressure you were still less able to find the words to address this child of yours, the child you were to see only once and then goodbye. Your ex-wife, less than three feet away, glares at you like the Queen of Hearts as she releases the hostility she'd stored and savored for eight long years.

I can see that little girl of yours, Katherine (?), curious and somewhat intimidated at the prospect of seeing her own father for almost the first time, about to speak to you, then clamming up suddenly, afraid her mother's anger is directed at her. Oh Phillip, my heart goes out to you and your daughter both. I am so glad the others took your side, and pressured Carole into agreeing to let you see Katherine one more time before the adoption, alone and without interference. Where did you take her? How did that meeting go? Please tell me things went all right that final time.

Rose.

I wanted to ask my father the same question: where did you go Dad, that one final afternoon you spent with the sister I never met? Did you go to the park? Swing on the swings the way you used to swing with me when I was nine?

How hurt you must have been that year I was gone and Dana had just started College. Five daughters and not one lived with you.

So Dina found the photographs.

That day in the park with Katherine, I was so close to my daughter, close for the first time, and yet I was afraid of touching her, of scaring her, of her not liking me, diffident, as with a newly acquired puppy, so much wanting to be friends.

Pete came along for support. He played with Kit easily, without embarrassment, side by side on the swings, as if he, perennial bachelor, had always lived among kids. "I have my nephews and nieces," he said. More reserved, I stood watching, ready to give a push, if needed, or to save a falling child.

We climbed and clambered over things. Katherine was a gawky long-limbed child. Large, dark brown eyes. She must be beautiful now. You could see something of my mother, of my entire family in her face, in the eyes and hair. At the very end of the afternoon, I took her into my arms and hugged her.

Do you remember, Dina, just before you ran away? Your mother found the marijuana in your purse and telephoned me. You'd left your purse open on the kitchen table waiting for it to be found.

I talked to your mom, while you stood there, fierce and determined. "She's got to agree to go to counseling with you. Or me. On a regular basis. Or we call the cops."

"Call them," you said, interrupting, hateful, "Call the cops, then."

"Dina, we just want you to talk with us."

"I'm getting out of here," you said and walked out the door.

I chased you down the stairs. You walked faster, not running, but getting away all the same across the lawns. I chased you down.

"Let go of me," you said.

I grabbed you, held you, hugged you to me.

"Let go of me," you said.

14. Letters to Aimai Cristen, Part II.

"Don't just read the letters higgledy-piggledy, sort them into categories."

I shook my head, puzzled, what did he mean?

Instead of answering, Dad slipped down on the floor beside me and reached into the box. "There are seven categories in all. Here's one: A good example of category 0 — the hopeless:"

> Dear Miss Cristen:
>
> I live alone in a three bedroom duplex.
>
> Things haven't gone well since my wife left.
>
> She took all the furniture. I use just the one room where the bed was and of course the kitchen to keep canned goods and such.
>
> It is quite a large house but it is empty now. I usually don't stay in it much except when I sleep. It is very lonely.
>
> You probably won't want to write to me.

"Of course, I don't want to write to him."

"I agree. He's hopeless." Dad paused and rummaged through the box. "Can't seem to find a Category 1. But they're all more or less the same: I am a stereo. Or, I am a '67 corvette, red, with mag wheels. They confuse themselves with the things they own.

"Ah. Here's a Category 2 — I am a penis."

"Dad!"

Dear Aimai: I'm sick and tired of chicks that only permit sex in the missionary position with the lights out. I'd love to find in you a mistress who if she doesn't revel in the exotic will at least try new things. I really dig a gal who loves to show off her body in the nude or filmy lingerie or exotics such as rubber and leather. We could have a ball trying out new positions, toys, costumes (both of us). Round the world, well that's a good start, how about vibrator tag, mistress and slave, nude showers, satin sheets, a bit of swapping, nothing to excess, I just want both is us to try out anything and find out what we can revel in. I'd like to get you some far out outfits for our evening together.

P.S. I'd send my photo, but I don't have a recent one, you won't be disappointed though.

"Pervert."

"Of course, some letters are more subtle."

Dear Aimai: Saw your rather unusual ad in the Barb and I must say I did not laugh at it, but thought it rather smart for it was a different way of catching a person's eye.

Just what are your interests, how old are you, not that it really matters. Please tell me about yourself, your likes and dislikes, whether you would be classified as a swinger or not, what you do, are like, and, it's really not important, what you like, hair, dementions etc

I am well off, money wise. I belong to the playboy club and drive a '68 car. I like to take polaroids and am a health nut I guess. I like all the cultures, French, Greek, Roman, and just love the Swedish Vine which really sends one out of this world.

I like exotic food and women, good shows, dancing, and sporting events. Now that you know me, tell me about yourself; also how about a picture. I am having one made and will return yours along with mine in my next letter if you so wish. Perhaps someday soon we might get together over lunch or supper or perhaps a drink or smoke even if it means off the grass as the saying goes.

Gross. I dropped the letter on the carpet and tried to forget I'd ever touched it. "A letter like this makes me feel covered with slime. How can you possibly rate it in a higher category than the one from a guy who told you all about his possessions?"

"At least a penis has something to do with being a human. Try having a Corvette hug you in the middle of the night."

"I'd kind of like a Corvette."

"Never mind .. Here's a Category 3 —awareness of self."

Dear Aimai: I have read your ad in the Berkeley Barb and it strike me your sincere which nowadays are very rare. I'm too looking for the kind of woman that you look to be. I love children and I do enjoy outgoings (picnics, days in the country, etc.)

I'm 28 years old, not good looking, but I'm warm hearted, gentle, and over all sincere and honest. I'm in the career of psychology and I've a masters degree in it. I enjoy talking and lots of time I go out in the mountains. I surely would like to know you, meet you and start our friendship. I'll wait your answer. Love from a person that considers himself your friend from now on.

"Category 4 is the con." my dad said.

"Remember the letter from the self-described 'Negro man?' The (his words) 'well-known business man around town. 'If you have any talent in entertainment, tell me about it. I'll get you in the next big show I bring to town.'

"Or maybe that other guy, the one who wrote about his intangible hopes, who wanted to work you into his plans. You'd marry his best friend and then the wife swapping could begin.

"The con artist knows there are other people out there, sort of. He just doesn't think of them as people."

My dad looked off into the distance, into his head again, before he spoke. "Actually, the wife-swapper seems to be maybe a half-step above the con artist. He had some empathy, after all, for Aimai and her needs.

"A lot of letters are sort of half-way between categories. Like the guy who writes that all bets are off if Aimai is a man. I mean, now that guy's not quite out of his self is he? So he's somewhere between a 3 and a 5, and I'd put him down below the con."

"What's a category 5?"

"My own letter, I guess; after all, she responded to it. And any letter that more or less dealt with her needs as well as the writer's, a letter that said, 'hey, there's a real person here, ready to share love, compassion, joy with you.'"

Dear Aimai:

I think I may have exactly what you need. My apartment in Brentwood is unoccupied most of the time and you are welcome to stay there.

My firm makes machine tools —I know, how boring. Our current emphasis is on building up European outlets and I've been spending more and more time abroad —Brussels and Paris, mainly. When I'm in town, I would be grateful if you'd let me serve as your escort. I like the theater and hope you do to. Though sometimes, I just enjoy a walk on the beach and dinner and a drink in a good restaurant —one with a view. The beach or the mountains, you choose.

Perhaps, you'd fly with me to Paris sometime.

I'm due back in town the 15th; let's talk.

Ciao. Bill.

"What a deal. Good thing you're letting me stay rent-free or I'd be off to Brentwood like a flash. Just kidding," I added when I saw the expression on his face, "And the last, highest category?"

"It's the letter we're all waiting for, from the person our father, mother should have been, the letter that says 'I'm here now. I see you exactly as you are and I want to be your friend.'"

"Will you be my friend, Dad?" But I didn't say this aloud.

15. Uncle Pete

My Uncle Pete is really not my Uncle, just an old friend of my father's. "I've known Pete since college," my dad says.

"Were you and my dad really roommates?" I asked Uncle Pete.

"Yes and no," he replied, tugging at his ear. (Pete's fingers were always busy; if he wasn't tugging at his ear, he was pulling at his hair or scratching his head.) "If you mean, did your dad and I split the rent, then the answer is no. I paid the rent; he crashed on the floor. If you mean, did your dad spend a lot of time at my place, even use it as kind of home away from home when he came to Berkeley, then the answer is yes. I know I gave him a key one time. And then I took it away from him when he didn't lock up properly."

"I've been in the same kind of trouble," I admitted.

"Well, I hope he has better luck with you, than I did with him. I mean taking away the key didn't seem to help. He'd let himself in anyway. I'd be gone for the weekend and find someone had eaten all the cereal. The least he could have done was replace it. He did buy milk, but that's only because I usually let the milk in my refrigerator hang around until it turned into yogurt mold or something."

We stay at my Uncle Pete's home whenever we're in the Bay area. I've spent at least five or six nights on the air mattress in Pete's apartment, I think all my sisters have.

I remember the first time we visited Pete. We were living in Michigan and my dad had brought me with him to the West Coast on a business trip. He always brought one of us kids with him whenever he made a trip. Dana got taken to Disneyland, Donna to Disney World, and I got taken to Berkeley.

My dad slept on a couch in Pete's living room and they got a camp cot for me. The next morning, they let me make my own cereal. This was the first time I had fixed my own breakfast. And I made breakfast for Dad and Pete, too, cornflakes and orange juice.

Pete said he liked the breakfast; cornflakes and orange juice was just perfect for him. But my dad said he wanted more and Pete and I could hear him stomping about in the kitchen cursing and saying, "Pete, where's your peanut butter?"

I hadn't had to ask Uncle Pete for anything. I'd found the cereal and I'd poured the milk by myself and Pete already had the sugar on the table.

Finally, my dad came back from the kitchen with two hunks of cheese on some burnt toast and made me eat one of the hunks. "You need protein," he said. And we each had another glass of milk. Pete says, "Where'd you get the cheese, I didn't even know I had it." Dad says "in the refrigerator." Pete says, "Wow, I must have bought that so long ago, I forgot about it." Dad says, "You did, I've been spending the last half hour in the kitchen scraping off the mold." Barf city, but I'd already eaten what Dad had given me.

Anyway, if I'd complained, my dad would have still made me eat it. He'd have said, it's O.K. if you scrape off the mold. I know, cause he's said it before. If my mom were around, she'd just say, "yes dear," and then as soon as Dad went off to his study, we'd throw the cheese out in the garbage. My mom used to do a lot of things like that when Dad wasn't watching. "He would drive me crazy otherwise," she'd say. I wish .. well, I wish she and Dad were still together. You'd think after eighteen years, with us kids practically grown and no trouble, they would have stayed together.

I mean, some people say that's the best part of marriage, when the kids are gone, when you no longer have to worry about them walking in when you're having sex, stuff like that. I remember one time, we hid out on the veranda, all three of us sisters, because we knew our parents were in the bedroom going "lovely, lovely," as Donna would say. Then, when we'd almost snuck into position to see something —Dana says she did see something —I got to giggling and that was the end of it. Dad was so mad, but he couldn't chase us very far because he wasn't wearing any clothes.

Anyway, after breakfast with Uncle Pete, Dad and I went to look for hiking boots, because Dad said these were what I needed for when we walked around the town. Dad said they sold things like that in Berkeley that were especially for kids. I've still got those boots somewhere. I can't believe I ever had feet that small. I don't think I wore the boots more than a couple of times after we got back home. Dad wanted me to wear them to school, but Mom said, no, Dina can wear running shoes at school if she wants to. And I wanted to because no one wore boots to school. I wore the boots in Berkeley, though, while we walked around, which was a good thing because my dad really likes to hike places.

Last week, I asked Uncle Pete what he knew about Dad's crazy days and he said, a lot more than he ever really wanted to:

"Your dad used to stay in my apartment when he was in Berkeley. He worked across the Peninsula at Missiles and Space, but he stayed at my place on the weekends. He even had a key at one time.

"I had to take it away from him when he.... But then, I already told you about that."

Pete paused for a moment, and scratched his head, as if uncertain whether to confide in me. For the first time, I noticed that his blond hair was thinning on top. Maybe it was all that scratching, or maybe baldness just ran in his family.

"Your dad is not very considerate. He does things and he doesn't think about their effects on those around him. Or he'll do something and imagine that because he wants to do it, you want to do it, too."

"And maybe you would," I stuck in, "if he'd just give you a chance to think about it."

"Exactly," said Pete. "Of all the selfish, self-centered things he did, I think the worst was when I looked in the Barb one Sunday and found he'd scheduled a psychodrama for that same afternoon in my apartment."

"He hadn't asked your permission?"

"We'd talked about it, but I hadn't said yes or no. I probably would have said no, if I'd known more about it. Anyhow, without telling me he put an ad in the paper: 'Psychodrama, 25 cents, 1011 Oxford, Sunday at 2pm.'"

"Twenty-five cents?!"

"Sounds silly, doesn't it. I asked your father, why twenty-five cents? And he tells me with a perfectly straight face, 'to keep out the riff-raff.'

"I think the idea was that he'd start small and gradually raise the fees as his Sunday afternoon sessions got popular.

"Anyway, it's Sunday afternoon, and I'm thinking maybe I should do something, go to my office or just go for a walk in the park —I hadn't read the Barb yet, when there's a knock on the door and this weird looking guy says he's there for the psychodrama. I told him I didn't know anything about it, when right behind him comes this couple —Dan and Ruth were their names —and they're asking about the psychodrama, too, only they've got the Barb ad with them. About this time, the telephone rings and it's your dad saying he's sorry he's late, but will I hold the fort until he gets there. I say, 'Phil wait a minute. You didn't ask my permission.' But you know how your dad is, he says, 'I'm sorry, I'll come right over and explain things to everybody.' Well, by the time he gets there, I've got maybe a half a dozen people in my living room.

"One of them is this very cute girl, Huldie something, so I'm not sure if I want them to go or not.

"Your dad wasn't at all repentant. He walks into my apartment likes he's walking on board his yacht and the first words out of his mouth aren't 'Gee, Pete, I'm sorry,' or 'Gee Pete, I should have asked your permission first,' but 'Did you collect the money?'

"I tell you, Dina, I was so mad, I could have spit. Right in front of everyone, I told him, "Phil, this is the last time you're ever going to use my apartment, O.K.'

"And what does your dad say? He turns to the people that have come for his psychodrama, smiles at them, and says, 'Would you like to work on your anger, Pete? That's what psychodrama is all about.'

"I took your dad by the arm and walked him outside. Putting my face about six inches from his face and, using a voice I would never have used with anyone else, I told him to hold his psychodrama, do whatever he needed to do, but if he even thought about getting me involved, I'd hit him. 'I'm not going to be your partner. I'm not going to be a guinea pig. I'm just going to watch.'

"And when I say this to him, my jaw is set. I can be real stubborn when I want to and he knew he meant it."

Uncle Pete's face reddened when he said this, and I knew he'd meant it. I changed the subject. "Exactly, what is a psychodrama?" I asked Pete.

"A good question," Pete said. "Well, I'm not a professional —I teach math, not psychology, but I'd say a psychodrama is something like what you get when you leave a fifth-grade class alone for five minutes without a teacher. People yelling, people running around screaming, throwing things, even hitting each other."

"Hitting each other?"

"Well, your father says they're not really supposed to hit each other, at least not destructively, but it's while he's teaching them how to hit each other in a non-destructive fashion that he gets punched in the nose.

"Afterward —he has to lead the entire psychodrama while he's lying on the floor, because every time he sits up his nose starts to bleed again —afterward he says to me, 'see how much control you can exert in the one-down position.'

"Anyhow, there's this one girl, Huldie, really cute, she's the main reason I didn't toss everybody out of my home in the first place, who says she's been having trouble relating to her father. So Phil has one of the guys take the role of her father and then Huldie and this 'father' start arguing in the middle of my living room. Oh, and whenever your dad hears one of the people in the psychodrama say something he thinks is phony, he crawls behind them—he still can't stand up because of the nosebleed, remember —and pretends to be them, saying what he thinks they should be saying. He encourages everyone to take sides, either by lining up behind Huldie and pretending to be her or by lining up behind her father, I mean, behind the kid who's pretending to be her father.

"Soon we've got half a dozen Huldies and half a dozen fathers and even one or two that are playing the role of Huldie's mother."

"And what are you?" I asked Pete.

"Me? I'm Peter Ross, the unwilling host to all this confusion. I'm standing in the kitchen doorway, and I stay right where I am till the psychodrama is over. I know how Phil is."

"So how did it end?"

"Let's see. This one really didn't end in any special way. It sort of went on until dark and then a lot of us, whoever was left, went off and had supper together. I know Scott was in my group and Dan and Ruth, the couple I was talking about. I think your dad stayed with Huldie.

"The psychodrama had a much more dramatic finish the following week. This time, they held it at Huldie's apartment —I wasn't about to let them back in my place —and your dad charges 50 cents apiece—big time."

"Same people as were at your house?" I asked.

"No, mostly new people. Huldie's there, of course. I'm there, only I'm not really there, because I'm still not going to get involved. Oh, and Dan and Ruth are back. They seemed to really enjoy what your dad was doing. They get in the middle of everything and they're always willing to be somebody's mother or somebody's husband. Usually they get on opposite sides. In fact, once or twice, they start screaming at each other, pretending to be say, Jim and Jim's ex-wife, and they go at it as if there were nobody else in the room."

"As if they were really Dan and Dan's wife Ruth having their usual quarrel."

"Exactly. Sounds as if you've been to one or two of these psychodramas yourself. What made this particular psychodrama at Huldie's memorable is that Huldie's father shows up midway through. Her *real* father. He's wearing a suit and everything. He wants to know what the hell everybody is doing in her apartment making all that noise. And when Huldie says she invited everybody, they're her friends; he says, well he's paying the rent and they've all got to go home. I mean it's a real psychodrama. Only Huldie's not telling her dad off, the way she does when some kid is pretending to be her father. She's not really saying anything, just kind of looking down at her shoe, the way most of us do in real life when somebody we're afraid of yells at us."

"Her dad was yelling?"

"Yes. This was the interesting part. He starts off very smooth, very controlled. He's wearing the suit, we're a bunch of beatniks, but soon he's screaming at his daughter, and he's screaming at Phil, and finally he kicks a hole in the wall of his apartment and stomps out.

96

"Not much anyone can say after that. No one can come up with a script that is that real. Still, no one leaves either; we all sit around and talk about our families. Even I started talking with this guy Scott about my family and that's something I don't usually do, not unless I've known someone for a long, long time. I suppose there's something to psychodrama after all, that is, if you can arrange to get the real parents together with the real children."

16. I Dig Rock & Roll Music

While searching for Aimai Cristen, Peter went to the Family Dog on the Great Highway where someone gave him a cap of psilocybin. This is how it began:

He was standing in the tail of a line which stretched two hundred yards along the highway in a direction opposite to Playland, when a girl, the girl on his right, asked him if he'd trade places with her. He made the exchange, only to discover that without the girl as a windbreak, the chill wind from the ocean blew directly across him. "Thanks," she said.

He was not amused. They advanced thirty or forty yards in stony silence before he noticed the line really wasn't moving forward; people were just clumping together for warmth. "It's going to take a long time," Peter said to no one in particular.

"I wonder where *they* are going?" the girl replied, pointing to four figures walking along the side of the theatre toward the rear. Peter looked at the vanishing foursome and then at the girl whose eye he had been avoiding. She wore a Japanese bathrobe, a yokata, patterned with chrysanthemums. Her hair, long and wild like that of a witch, seemed to suit the costume. He looked away toward the ocean again and shivered. He should have brought a jacket.

Three of the figures returned from the rear of the theatre. They might have been the same persons he'd seen a moment ago or they might have been quite different ones. The ticket office still seemed far away and unattainable, the line unmoving. "One of the boys didn't come back," Peter said to the girl, "do you want to chance it? We could ask these people to hold our place."

He and the girl struck off across the sands, a careful distance between them. The night was moonless; the ocean hid all sounds. Two men were coming out of a compound at the rear of the theatre rolling what might have been a tank of compressed air. They rolled the tank up the ramp of a pickup truck, folded the ramp away, then locked the fence carefully behind them.

"Damn," said Peter who'd been watching the entire procedure closely, waiting for an opportunity to slip inside. He and the girl continued walking. They followed the fence back and around the corner to where the compound ended. Here, the top of the fence was on a level with the rising ground. Below, in a courtyard, seventy or so persons milled about happily, the lucky ones who had come early before the line had formed. To join them, he and the girl would have to climb out on a fragile wooden trellis, then risk a drop of twenty feet.

Further on, the ground dropped away behind a concrete wall that appeared to run the full length of the building. An opening appeared suddenly, a green door set in a niche in the wall. Peter pulled on the handle. The door did not budge.

Midway along the wall, the complex divided into three structures —the patio in back of them where the crowds still milled about noisily, the theatre, itself, and a set of detached dressing rooms to the theatre's rear. They stumbled finally upon the corridor that separated the theatre from the dressing rooms and ran along it, attracted by the lights ahead.

The corridor ended in two clear glass doors. Ahead of them, they could see the line metering in from the front of the building. Peter tapped on the glass but no one responded. They might as well have been invisible. Before Peter could think of a plan, a high-pitched male voice said, "I can't let you in."

The man in the flowery blue robe looked apologetic. "Just a party of two, just two of us," Pete stammered.

The man could look down the long empty corridor and see that what Peter said was true. "O.K. Wait a moment till the guy inside looks the other way. . . now shoot."

Peter and the girl leaped through the doorway and merged into the crowd. Pete paused once he felt his disappearing act was complete, but the girl kept moving deeper into the theatre. (Hey, he thought, I don't know her name.) "Hey" he said, "I don't know your name."

The girl stopped. "It's Marsha." She started off again, and then turned back. "I've got to meet my old man," she apologized. "Oh, Gee. You thought. . . . Take this will you." She pressed a capsule into his hand.

100

"Huh." Pete stared stupidly at the capsule.

"Take it," the girl, Marsha, said, "Put it in your mouth."

Peter put the capsule in his mouth and swallowed it without meaning to. The girl waved as she skipped off. This was how Peter came to take psilocybin.

. . . "There's a lot of dope going down here."

"I knew from the way she was acting, from the way, you know, holding her head like that . . . ."

"All the heads . . ."

"Janice, where did you put my slipper?" . . .

Pete went downstairs to go upstairs to a balcony that ran the length of the auditorium. He became part of a crowd trying to look over or around the pile of equipment which belonged to the light show crew—stands, mirrors, oil cans, plastic squeeze bottles, dishes, projectors and a huge transparent screen.

A color wheel circled before one of the projectors as the opposite wall changed from blue to green to red and back. A drop of brown grew and grew until it had captured the remaining yellow and then, in turn, was displaced in a shower of pink.

"Pig: oink, oink, oink," read a set of dictionary definitions projected on the screen. "Pig" turned into "knio, knio, knio :giP" as the light crew flipped the slide from back to front.

Pete would have liked to sit down, but there were no chairs. When he leaned against the wall, the shifting crowds blocked his view. He tried squatting on his haunches closer to the center of the room, but found this position uncomfortable too.

The people disturbed him, he admitted. They were younger, more aggressive . . . different. Moustaches and sideburns proclaimed their identity. Their hair was uniformly long and greasy. Their outfits were mismatched, western shirts with bell-bottoms, or dress pants and sneakers.

A brown-skinned boy near him wore a turban and a Nepal tunic, but there was something right about him, about everyone in costume, like the short, pretty girl in 15th century Elizabethan dress, whose skirts lifted about her as she walked. The Americans who dressed as Americans in a sweater or T-shirt made him feel uneasy.

Uneasy? Where? On Peter's right side just below the last rib, a tic in the muscle pulled him sideways away from eye-to-eye contact.

On second thought, the two t-shirt clad youths who pushed passed him were just having fun. He laughed with them, at them. They were really quite funny.

The guitars had given way to an unaccomplished saxophone player. He fought with his instrument, its wha-wha sound emerging over amplified and distorted from the speakers on both sides of the hall. Peter had learned to play the saxophone slowly, almost painfully. He did not play it often. And never without trying or caring.

"What's the matter with you?" the cat said. "Your face is all squinched up as if you'd been eating lemons."

"I was just thinking . . ." Peter slurred, "Who are you? You're . . . weird."

Brown eyeliner had created a cat's mask with slanted feline eyes and long brown whiskers. Pussy wore a Japanese yokata patterned with chrysanthemums; her long, witch-like hair had a white streak down its center. "Marsha," he exclaimed, placing the face at last, "Did you find your old man?"

"Him! Let's get some food."

"Sure," Pete said, following Marsha as closely as he could down the stairs and out onto the patio they'd looked down on earlier. The mock Playboy mansion held a fireplace, concrete benches near a terraced waterfall, a group gathered about a piano —their mouths were opening and closing but no sounds emerged—and, opposite the waterfall, what must be tables of food. Peter salivated as he saw the plates being passed from hand to hand —chicken, garlic bread, potatoes.

Pete was given a plate of beans. He was disappointed. Marsha had been given a plate of beans, too.

"Give yours away," Marsha suggested. She fed him from her own plate, moving her hand to and fro in time with the music. Pete arched his back and craned his neck back and forth like a cobra trying to lick the fork. Marsha giggled.

"Like this," she said and showed him how to move his head back and forth on a single plane like a Balinese dancer.

"Like this?" Pete folded his neck in the wrong direction each time his head popped out.

Marsha giggled. "You look like a drunken geisha girl."

The music grew louder, more frenetic as a roll of drummers was unleashed on the patio. The music caught at his limbs, yet Peter danced as if his heels were glued to the pavement. He couldn't get unstuck. He was like a paper frog tucked and folded in on itself.

"You're no fun," said Marsha.

He'd tried, he told himself, suddenly depressed. "I only am if you want me to be."

Marsha put her hand in his. They walked hand in hand back inside to where they were caught up in the wonder of the Cleanliness and Godliness Skiffle Band—guitars, drums, an organ, and a microphone taped to a sax. They worshiped the magic of the number 3 displayed in all forms and all languages superimposed on the swirling colors. The tone of the Moog synthesizer began high in the air; it grew inside them and ended in a series of thunderous vibrations that shook the floor. "Wow," they said, knowing what it was to be stoned.

"Is the stuff getting to you?" Marsha asked.

"I don't know. I was wondering? How long does the drug take? What does it do? What . . . ?"

"You're stoned, all right."

"No, no!" he said, but the sounds were all in his brain.

They sat on the floor, another island amid the couples and groups watching the Mime troupe perform the tale of Black Panther and Little White Fuzz and, later, the story of Uncle Tom's Ghetto. They stood up while they sat and walked hand in hand in the rim of the great wheel.

The Moog synthesizer played again and the light show licked out from the screen with sudden burpings of its strobe. Peter was happy, happier at a party than he'd ever been before.

"I want some water," Marsha said. "Don't you want some water?"

Peter opened his mouth to lick the rain.

A petite flower child hovered by his shoulder, "All that comes out of the faucet is a trickle; you'll have to put your head down next to it." Peter looked at her and thanked her with his smile, a radiant wonderful smile that lit up the people on either side of him. His head was heavy and he let the child hold it in her hands and touch his hair.

Marsha also held him, by the arm, keeping him in the line for water. The line was long. The scene changed from night to day each time the light show crew tripped a switch or the door to the men's room opened.

(I could get a drink in there, Peter thought, from my outstretched arm and hand held beneath the faucet's flow. By turning, bringing the right foot back before the left, before I talk to Marsha, then moving toward the men's room after explaining to her where to wait, taking a forward step with the right foot in a place where, after I've come back, after I've taken the drink and, if there were only a few people in the room, say, after I had turned easily and freely away from the urinals, to the right if they were on the left and the door of the room were on my right, taking a step . . . .)

"Oh, God," Peter thought or said out loud, "I'd better just wait here in line."

Marsha's lips went to the spigot. She inhaled the fluid hung motionless above the fountain. Behind them a drum welcomed people to the Fair.

("We'll be late," he thought.) "You can get a drink now," she said.

He bent to the fountain, touched his lips in agreement. Marsha ran to catch up with him.

The colors rippled through the walls. He heard the music. He could dance. Then, at that instant, he knew each part of his body: he knew which muscles moved when he walked and when he raised his hand. He felt the air on his fingertips.

"I know now," he said to Marsha. "I know whichhandand how we movethe partofthemeaning inthelegIam."

Peter stopped speaking, knowing he couldn't, and smiled. He was part of a group around the piano that stood with their arms draped over each other's shoulders. They were all together: the boy in the blue with the beads, the man who'd dished out the food, the actor and the poet.

". . . to sit down." Marsha said and guided
him away from the crowd to a bench. They were
alone there, terribly alone. The parquet stretched
off endlessly before reflections of themselves
could be seen sitting in the distance. "Not here!"
he whimpered.

She took him to sit by the fountain, which
gurgled. They were alone there, too, but it was all
right. There was fog. Marsha sipped the fog with
her tongue. He opened his mouth and drank heavily
from the condensing vapor.

"You won't quench your thirst very quickly that
way," she said, "it will take you a month."

(Doesn't Marsha understand, Peter thought, how
useless it is to . . . to reason.) He dipped his
hand into the wishing pool and drank.

"I don't think you should," she said.

"Recirculating?"

"Recirculating."

Peter tried to spit out the dirty water but
could only drool. He shook his slime-covered hand
helplessly. "Watch over me," he pleaded, "Watch
over me."

Marsha led them back inside to where she said
it would be warm and they could sit down. Peter
was cooperative, but kept shutting his eyes and
falling down.

"Lean against me," she said. "No, you can't
lean there. I've got to have something to lean
against, too. Hold yourself up for a moment. O.K.
Now, you can lean on me. Oh, now you don't want
to."

Peter and Marsha sat on the end of the platform that held the musicians. He rocked in time with the music, thinking:

this can't go on much longer, is it over, there is no time, i might be insane, i am insane if the concert is over and still i am GO WITH IT knowing that it might have been just so much time since we stood in line outside the theatre, Marsha and me, have Marsha remind me afterwards of how it was, the ebb and flow, this experience smiling, friends, closer than those he used to work with, friends, liking and relating, friends, human beings.

Next to Peter on the stand there sat a Mexican boy. The boy seemed oblivious to what Peter was or what he had become. The boy looked out at the crowds much as Pete

who danced with the others in the market place, old friends, the baker and the priest; Emilio fed his fat wife with a spoon; simple people, good people;

who thought, it's all lies; they are just wearing costumes, torn cloth and fake hats; is it getting worse or better? how did it start? when was the moment when GO WITH IT che coo churaha.

Next to Peter on the stand sat a Mexican boy. The boy seemed oblivious to what Peter was or had become. The boy looked out at the crowds much as Pete had been doing.

The Mexican boy smiled. Nervously? not nervously.

"Are you a Mexican?" Peter asked.

"Yes."

(Now I know, thought Peter, letting himself slip once more into the carnival mood. Just costumes. The dead men are out of place. The man talking to the other with his hands is not a narcotics agent but a tourist.

Did I ask the boy?)

His head plopped loosely on Marsha's thigh. He pressed against her. He was happy.

"Poster."

Peter blinked stupidly at the poster he now held. The Mexican boy held a poster, as did the man beyond him, and the man beyond that. With one glance Peter saw words: "while you are studying," pictures of barren parks, "give," and pictures of starving children.

mouths begging him for food; drifting in the wind, torn scraps of paper; the food unwrapped and rotting on the barren ground. He looked up as the children came toward him, eyes beseeching, mouths open, their jaws gaping, hungry! He clung to Marsha, burying his face in the fold of her blouse. He closed the hungry faces out, only to reopen his eyes and see the frail grey bodies cast off on his left.

(crying) Peter was not crying for no tears came. (Marsha was gone far away. Marsha could not stay to feed him.) "I can't breathe, I can't breathe."

(He was all right. Marsha would be there.) "Will you watch over me to see that I breathe?"

(Did Marsha hear that? Had he said it aloud?)
He fell forward in a sticky mass of yellow and gray
feathers, blood oozing from fresh wounds.

Marsha looked up. "We've got to go," she
said.

(oh, no!) Peter rocked to and fro in his
agitation. (Not leave! My friends. My friend the
Chicano.) He touched the Mexican boy's thigh and
smiled. The Mexican smiled back at him as Marsha
rose stiffly.

She tugged at Pete's arm. "We've got to go."
She sounded just like his mother.

"Like my mother," thought Peter rolling back
and forth and giggling.

"Oh, my God," Marsha exclaimed as the stage
crew swarmed onto the platform and started setting
up the props around them. The lights came on in
the puppet theatre to their right and the voice of
Punch could be heard threatening and cajoling as
Marsha led Peter away.

"He won't like this," Marsha announced to no
one in particular.

(Won't like it. Won't like it.) He stopped
thinking about his feet and the prospect of moving
and just let go.

"Whoops, hold on there."

He fell across the spread thighs of an obese
blond. She looked as if she didn't know whether to
laugh or cry. Finally, she turned away though
Peter continued to remain on and beside her
giggling. And giggling.

Then he cried.

Marsha looked up, a hand before her face as if to ward off evil. "What's wrong?"

"Won't like this." Peter wailed.

"Are you sane enough to move?" she asked. She thought: we'll have to move and he can't walk; I can't carry him; he'll just fall over and grin.

Somehow or other he walked. Soberly. Taking little snapshots of the room with his eyes. (My God, he thought wistfully, I've come down.)

A girl sat near the doorway to the patio, a warty girl with acne-riddled cheeks. She sat in a window niche crooning to a lap harp. A single note emerged from the harp, a single golden note that seemed to last for all eternity. He knelt before a golden throne. The air was wine, the note was crystal. A single golden note hung timeless in a single eternal moment. The room, the theatre was life.

"Oh! Oh, I'm sane. I've lost it. Let me go back, go back."

The girl with the harp continued to play and chant. Others joined her lending strained voices to an unmusical wail.

(In the market, the musicians played. The rich tossed coins. Stern Cossacks, fresh from their horses, pungent with the mingled sweat of man and horse, trooped between the stalls. The oriental merchants patted their global bellies, bit coins behind their smiles. A single turbaned Arab guided the progress of sixteen Circassian dancing girls, each heavy with scent and full of laughter.)

"You want to sit down?" Marsha asked.

(No. No. Not to leave before they'd bought, bought . . . gone back to the moment when... when ... two bellicose hunters from the mountains still swaddled in their furs ... a Nubian slave with his mistress' treasure, iridescent bottles formed of rippling glass . . .)

"You won't sit down, you won't stand up."

One of the blacks took his hand: "This your girl, man?"

Peter looked up into the negro's face and giggled. The black went away.

"You beat them off with a smile," Marsha said. "You're some lover, you know that?"

Peter clung to her. The patio was filled with other couples, joining: a hug with head to torso, arms around the waist and up the body's sides; a frail girl in the crook of a strong man's arm. He saw himself within the circle, held of her/him. Part of knowing was to be held.

A boy stared at Peter with eyes that were rigid and protruding. (He knows, Peter thought.) An aged oriental returned Peter's gaze benignly. (He too knows; but though one knows and one knows, it is not the same way of knowing.)

Marsha shivered on the concrete bench, finding little warmth in her yokata. Peter clung to her, moaning in ecstasy. (We've got to go inside, she thought. If I have to drag him.

God. That means we'll have to go by that horrid girl again —the one with the harp, droning. Those people who joined her, where on earth did

112

they come from? Shaved skulls, that whole Hare Krishna crowd, ugh. I wonder what he thinks of them?

You won't tell me anything will you? Just look up at me and grin.)

She led Peter back across the patio, past the fountain waters dripping from terrace to terrace. (People strolled through the market as before, but they bought less. Their costumes were soiled, the hems dirt encrusted. The swarthy, dark-haired girl stroked her instrument sadly, soundlessly. It was not as it had been before. Not at all. He wanted to rush away; but first; he would have to rest.)

Marsha had Peter lean against the window. (There were people trapped inside beating with their fists on the pane.) "Marsha, the people!" he cried.

(Oh, God, she thought. You won't go on; you won't let go of me. It's cold out here.) "Just hold me will you?"

He held her and the great arc of the universe carried them away in a dance.

"Here," Marsha said. (No, no, he thought, seeing the window, the outside, the wheeling stars, thinking to fall and fall.)

"Where are you taking him?" someone asked.

"The balcony."

"You'll never make it. How stoned is he?" the same voice persisted.

"I wish I knew."

"THE POETS," boomed the loudspeaker.

"They say Haight Street is dead.

Well it is dead.

Hate is dead.

All is love."

(Dead, dead, dead; the crowd writhed and tore and
twisted around them like something evil barely
suggested in a fun-house mirror.

But

Peter was love

that touched them

anointed them.)

   "You've got to keep moving," Marsha said as
Peter's stares were returned.

   Peter would be moving and Marsha would be
stopped. Marsha would want to move just when the
pattern on the TV set had reformed the crowd on new
lines. Peter took step after step running while
Marsha held him, knees just off the floor.

   "Marsha?"

   "Yes?"

   "Is it you?"

   She had found them a resting place in the
alcove under the stairs. The alcove was hot and
stuffy, but she was grateful for its sanctuary.
Their only view of the light show was reflected and

114

intermittent and the voices of the poets were
muffled.

"I'm cold," Peter said.

"No, you're not." (When he's outside, he's
warm; when he's inside, he's cold.)

"The cables . . . electric . . . danger . . .
want to move," he told her.

(Sure you do; three feet and you'll collapse.)

"Is he dead?" Peter asked.

It was a reasonable assumption. The individual
in question lay stretched out on the floor, his
neck bent at the junction of the floor and the wall
as if broken. His comatose position was no longer
unusual; the concert had degenerated and half-
asleep participants were sprawled everywhere. (How
much longer would the damn poets gerbil, she
wondered?)

Peter pressed his lips to Marsha's waist. How
wonderful she was. It was all wonderful, the
party, the noises when the crackers popped and now
the favors. At midnight, there would be balloons
breaking and crepe paper streamers would drop
falling and spinning, falling and spinning.
Wherever Marsha and he went to dance, in whatever
Bishop's castle, they would always be happy.

"Marsha?"

"Yes?"

"You're Marsha," he said.

"Yep, I'm her all right."

"The cables?"

"No problem."

He seemed to be sleeping. The poets droned on.
Periodically, he would jerk upright, mumble
something about the cables, then let his head fall
back in her lap. Marsha's old man found them thus
in the corner.

"Who is this?"

(Who am I, Peter thought, oh who am I?)

"He's stoned."

"Yup."

Light swirled inside Peter and bathed Marsha's
head in a Madonna-like glow. The great wheel
carried them together through the auditorium.

Her fanny was beginning to ache. The concert
had gone on much too long.

"He's asleep," Peter said. Marsha could not
be sure whom, if anyone, he was talking about.
"Yes, he's asleep," she said.

"Those cables, suppose I pull them down?"

"You won't. Let's go for a walk, huh."

"We won't go outside?"

"Where it's warm? C'mon. Up, up, up.
Smile."

"I'm smiling." He gave a wan smile that
brought tears to his eyes even as, head lolling, he
responded to yet another internal fantasy.

"Sure you are, baby. All night long."

"I love you, Marsha."

"O.K." The cat-face grinned.

The audience, those still on their feet, staggered about the huge, barn-like auditorium. The last of the poets spat into a dead microphone. Music stopped and started at random as each new volunteer found the turntable.

The tide had ebbed. Flaming essences spun out from the crowd, drifted like white flecks of foam out the doors to the parking lot and were gone. Peter wanted to walk with Marsha, to love Marsha.

"This concert is really degenerating."

(Degenerating. The German eagle flashed again and again on the screen. A huddle of black-leather jackets hid other prostrate forms. The Angels' blond mamas had puffy beer-reddened, satanic faces.)

"Do you want to come down?" came a voice, not Marsha's.

(Was the voice from outside him? I don't want to come down. They could be lying puppy-like, warm and loving, amid the heaped banquet cushions.

Remember. Remember the dancers in brief costumes of forest green. Remember the flute songs.)

"Step down," the voice insisted.

They'd come to the same stairway leading from the building that had scared him so before. But now, through the long window facing the great highway, he could see the planets. They moved in stately majesty across the sky — Jupiter and Saturn and Mars. . . .

"Was there a fight?" a male voice asked.

"Just somebody freaked out, that's all."

"Can't you get him to come home?" Marsha and her boyfriend bent over Peter. A group of freaks were dancing nearby. Marsha's boyfriend seemed afraid they'd be drawn in to the dancing and annoyed at his own fears.

"Did we dance?" Pete asked Marsha.

"Sometimes, baby. When you didn't fall over."

Peter smiled, remembering the dances . . . holding Marsha, having the beat inside him. His gaze wandered about the room and across the ceiling until it fixed on the light show opposite. He could look inside the pictures and be part of a spaceship yearning for the planets.

"Don't you want to come home?"

Peter wanted to shake his head, "No." He plotted as rapidly as he could till his thoughts slowed to the pace of speech. He smiled cunningly, "Can we come back afterwards and watch the light show?"

"Don't worry about it," Marsha's boyfriend said harshly, "You've got your own light show."

Peter let himself be led away from the building. His head hung uselessly, though he kept trying to use it to look back, kept trying to remember.

It ought to have been cold. But there were bright lights hanging from the closed hot dog stands, and a warm wind blew in from the ocean. He wanted to watch the lights but they came back for him and urged him forward.

118

"Baby, I'm so cold," Marsha wailed, pulling her damp bathrobe about her; she clung to Peter shivering, huddling within the shelter of his arms. The fog beat down upon them in great droplets, thunder and lightning from passing cars.

The wind howled. "Is anyone going to Berkeley, Berkeley?"

(They were alone and without food. He had to have food. Each person had to have food to live.

He looked upon the breadlines of unemployed engineers and Ph.D.'s, a thin ribbon in the swirling carnival madness.)

"Food," said Peter.

"Car? Where's your car?" they kept asking him. Finally, he pointed to one. "Good thing it's unlocked," they said.

(I never leave my car unlocked, thought Peter.) But they left him inside it, propped up in the passenger seat, anyway.

San Francisco, 1969.

About Dancing

"One thing, I'd like to know about," I said to my father after I'd finished reading his story, "You may think my question is a little off-the-wall, though."

Dad grunted which I took to mean he was listening. Our eyes met for an instant and, again, I looked away first. "Did you dance at these rock concerts, I mean, were people able to get up and dance near the stage, the way we do today sometimes?"

"Of course, we danced. None of this namby-pamby take-the-money and damm-the-public Milli-Vanilli stuff where you are forced to sit in predesignated seats or where a group of Nazi storm troopers herd you out of the aisles and off the stage.

"I mean, there weren't any seats at the Family Dog or at the Shrine Auditorium, which was almost the same sort of place only down in L.A. I saw Janis twice at the Shrine. You sat down or you danced. There weren't any seats at Woodstock. People could get up and walk around and be with their friends or make new ones. None of this business of limiting the guy in seat R43 to the cellmates the computer assigned to seats R44 and R42. You know, at my first concert, an Angel, an Hell's Angel, just lifted up the fence and in I walked.

My Dad took a deep breath. "Of course, we danced. Down front, by the stage, in the corridors or loose on the grass. To the music. You didn't have to move your hips in some special way or walk through a box step. Just go with the flow. And you didn't have to have a partner, all you had to do was get up and dance."

"That's the way we do it today," I interrupted, "When Jenny, and MeLi and I and maybe Bobbie and Danny go dancing, we'll all dance together in a group."

120

"And sometimes one group will merge with another," my father continued, "and you'll find yourself dancing next to somebody who's really neat and maybe you'll go sit down next to them for awhile."

"We don't do much of that," I confessed.

"We did then. It's a lot less embarrassing to meet another person that way, than to have to walk across a dance floor and ask a strange girl to dance while all her friends are looking at you. You're thinking, 'oh what if she says, no, and all these people will look at me like I'm some kind of a dork.'"

"That's why we dance in a group," I said. "Nobody is left out, and you don't need to feel embarrassed whether you're asking someone or no one is asking you."

"Huh. Sounds like the kids always get it right. You know, in my age group, we're back to dancing with a partner and you still have to take that long lonely walk to where the girl is sitting and say, 'Will you dance this dance with me?'"

"You don't need to worry. You're a good dancer Dad."

"Thanks. I don't get turned down too often. It's the dance lessons. I started taking dance lessons with your mom to begin with. Thought it was going to save my marriage.

"You know, you read about how each generation has its own style of dancing. They do and they don't. It's more a question of age. When I was sixteen, everyone danced in couples. Well, not everyone, a lot of us were scared to take a girl in our arms. Girls have bumps. When I was twenty-five, we danced in groups and the best way to meet people was with a smile. That's the way you and Dana dance today."

"Yeah, but Donna's the one who always has a date."

He beamed. He was very proud of Donna. About her being so popular. He'd always liked Donna, yet she was the one who badmouthed him the most. When mom and dad were breaking up I mean. I didn't want to write about that. Why am I writing about that?

"She's a great dancer," Dad said. He was still talking about Donna. "The way she picks up those steps. Show her something once and she knows it for ever."

I should have interrupted him then and said something about me. How difficult I find it sometimes to do the step and talk to my partner and keep to the beat. "You're a great dancer, too Dad," I said. I was telling the truth, but mainly I was hoping he would say something flattering about my dancing in return. I was hoping he would stop talking about Donna and start talking about me. He was right about Donna though, show her a dance step once and she knew it.

"You know why I look good dancing?" he said, "I'm not a natural dancer. Not like Donna. But I've practiced. I've practiced every step you see me do over and over 2000 times."

"2000 times," I echoed even as I felt despair at the challenge and excited by the possibility.

About Drugs

"The Peter in this story, is that Uncle Pete?" I asked my Dad.

"No, that's me. Peter is an alias."

"Then you used drugs."

"A drug. Psilocybin. And it's not a drug in the sense that cocaine or smack are. It's an hallucinogen, like mescaline or lysergic acid."

"What's the difference?"

"'Turquoise horses, a house made of dawn.' Psilocybin is not addictive. You're not going to wake up the next morning and want more because you miss the rush. Psilocybin, mescaline, they're like going on a trip. When you get back from Mexico, you don't feel as if you've got to go rushing off to Hawaii. No, you're going to wait until

122

you've developed the pictures you took, and you've had a chance to show them to your friends. You'll want to catch up on your laundry and start the newspaper up again. With psilocybin or any of the hallucinogens, it's the same way. The drug has such a mind-blasting effect, you're not likely to want to use it the next day or the next week. You spend a long interval thinking over what you learned on the last trip before you venture on a new one."

"What about the flashbacks you're supposed to get after you use acid?"

"The same flashbacks you get with any intense emotional experience. How many times since your grandmother's death have I thought about her, started talking, even turned around to hear her reply, then grieved because she was no longer there to talk with me. There wasn't any drug involved"

"So you think I ought to try some."

"I think you ought to feed your head. The more knowledge, the more images you have inside you when you take a hallucinogen, the more rewarding your trip will be."

"Feed your head?"

"Like the Dormouse said: White Rabbit, the song Grace Slick wrote, it's on the Airplane's Surrealistic Pillow album.

"You know, kid, there are three basic rules if you're going to use drugs." He paused. "Never follow a downer with a downer; never follow an upper with an upper; and feed your head.

"And you know what the first and most important rule is? Respect yourself."

That's four, I thought, but decided to let it go. I didn't need another lecture. "What's a downer?"

"Something that brings you down, a drug with a sedative effect like alcohol, or Quaaludes, or heroin. You probably knew that already, at last intuitively. But let's not change the subject, Princess. That's one of the minor rules. The biggies are feed your head and respect yourself.

"I do respect myself. That's why you call me princess."

"Touché," he said and flashed me the thumbs up sign. He grinned.

About Aimai Cristen

Dad's story had begun, 'While Peter was looking for Aimai Cristen.' And he'd said that in this story, he was Peter. Had he really been looking for her?

"Yes. I looked for her at rock concerts and at Human Be-Ins. I looked for her when I walked down the street in the Haight-Asbury or visited somebody on a houseboat in Sausalito. I'd look for her out of the corner of my eye. I knew if I looked for her directly I wouldn't find her. She'd as much as told me she was planning on disappearing, going off with this 'brother' of hers."

Suddenly, it all made sense to me. No, not the story my father had written about the rock concert, but how this person who was my father, Dr. Good, Calloway Professor of Computer Science, could also have been an underground reporter and dropped acid and answered ads in the Barb.

"You really didn't belong in the sixties, did you?" I said to him.

"What do you mean, not belong? I was a Barb reporter, a free-U instructor. I organized freedom rides."

"Yeah, but you really didn't experience any of these things. You couldn't just go to a human be-in as a human being, you had to be looking for Seri Cristen or covering the event for the Barb.

"You couldn't just be a spectator. Like, when we kids were playing soccer, you had to be a coach or a referee, you couldn't just be a Dad. You always have to be the hero of your own little play."

124

"They call that sort of behavior hypo-manic today. And they give you Lithium," he said, trying to turn away the truth of what I was saying with a joke.

But I wasn't going to let him get away with the evasion: "I call it not being willing to sit and enjoy your own kid. Whether she scores a goal or not. Whether she dribbles the ball the right way or not. You always had to critique everything we kids did. You couldn't just be content with, 'I enjoyed watching you play, Dina,' or 'wasn't that an exciting run!' or even, 'I could see how difficult it was for you to get your breath.' I could see you on the sidelines, Dad, explaining things to people. You know how many times I wanted you to turn around and watch me, Dad. Just watch me."

There. I'd said it to him. Finally. What I think I'd come back home to say. There was a long pause.   Time enough for him to think about what I'd said, time enough for me to wonder if I should have said it. And then he spoke. "Hi."

I looked at him blankly.

"Hi. Your hair looks good."

"Oh yeah, I was trying blond streaks again."

"I'm a plain vanilla man myself, but on you, streaks look good."

"I'm not asking for a critique Dad. I told you."

"You . . look . . good," he repeated, emphasizing each of the three words.

"O.K. Thank you."

"You're welcome." His eyes were locked on mine. It was a start.

17. Burglary

I was talking to my Uncle Pete. "You said to me once that Dad used to stay overnight with you when he was in Berkeley. Where did he stay the rest of the time? I know he lived for awhile in L.A., he told me about that, but where did he live after he moved up here?"

Pete blushed and stammered. He's like that a lot of the time, so I knew the answer would probably have something to do with sex. "Frankly," he said, "a lot of the time your father didn't really have a place of his own. Oh, a room maybe in which to store his things. I know that when he was in the Bay Area, he lived with Sandra in Palo Alto some of the time, but he also lived with Joan upstairs, and with some girl in the city who was working on her Ph.D. in clinical psych."

"Joan?" I questioned.

"Yeah. She was one of my next door neighbors, the 'upstairs girl' we called her; she was the one that got burglarized."

"Tell me about her. No, tell me about the burglary."

"Oh, that's a good story. And it has nothing to do with the cat. Your father is in it, too."

I motioned with my hand for Pete to go ahead and tell me.

"Your father was staying overnight in Joan's apartment. I didn't know he was there; I just knew that he was around, because I'd seen his car parked on the street. Of course, he could have just parked there and walked over to somebody else's place."

I held up my hand like a traffic cop. "Pete. Tell me about the burglary."

"A robbery, really, because the people were home. Well, it turns out Joan had this wanna-be boyfriend. Or maybe I should tell it from the beginning. Phil and Joan are asleep. Joan's place is a studio apartment like mine was then, so the bed is in the living room. She was going to have a bath and had poured the bathwater, but then Phil came over."

"Pete. Tell about the burglary."

"The bathwater is important. This wannabe boyfriend decides at four in the morning that he's going to come visit Joan."

"He's done that before?"

"He's never even had a date with her. He just sort of hung around her at the University, hinting, without really asking her out or anything. So at four in the morning, he crawls into her apartment through the bathroom window, steps on the edge of the tub and — this is the important part —steps over the tub without stepping into the bath water. No one could ever figure out how he did it, especially in the dark.

"He walks into the living room, turns on this big flashlight and shines it on the bed. Phil wakes up, sees the flashlight shining in his face and says to himself, 'Cop.' What's a cop doing there, your dad wants to know. Then, he gets mad at this cop just breaking in without knocking, so he leaps out of bed and starts to punch and hit this guy just as if he'd been studying karate.

"My dad doesn't know karate."

"I know. Your dad starts punching this guy and the guy steps back and knocks over a lamp. Joan hears the noise and wakes up. Next, they knock over the record player. The guy swings at your dad and your dad swings at the guy. They step on a table and break it. They destroy a chair. When Joan finally turns on the light, there isn't a piece of furniture in the room that isn't broken, except for the bed.

"Now, your father knows I lives downstairs and he begins to holler, 'Pete, help, help!' I wake up and I hear someone hollering, 'Pete, Pete.' But I'm real groggy —I probably didn't get to sleep until two, and you know how you are when you first go to bed. I get up —I'm in my pajamas —and I go upstairs. The door to Joan's apartment opens and this guy comes out. His nose is swollen, his shirt is ripped, and he's only wearing one shoe. Phil follows after him a moment later. Phil usually wears pajamas to bed or he used to, but all he's got on now are a few strips of cloth. Your dad sees me and he hollers, 'Watch him, Pete. Watch him.' Then, your dad goes back in the apartment. I watch as the guy goes shuffling off down the street, he's only wearing this one shoe and can't move very fast. Your dad comes back out on the landing then and says, 'Pete, where'd he go? You were supposed to watch him.'

We both laughed, though for a moment I was not really sure Pete was aware of the joke. "Did they catch the wannabe boyfriend?" I asked.

"Oh sure, that's how they found out he was a professor at the University. He didn't get very far, maybe a block, before the police pulled him over. There aren't that many guys running around the street at four in the morning with only one shoe on."

"And they can't run very fast."

"Your dad was sure mad at me, though. 'Why didn't you watch him, Pete?' he kept saying over and over. And of course, Joan's apartment was a complete mess. The guy and your dad had destroyed everything during the fight: furniture broken, record player smashed, the bookcase tipped over, and the gold-fish bowl that used to be on top spilled all over the sofa."

18. Two Girls, One Night in Hawaii

Like Charlie Brown, I knew a little red-haired girl in the first grade. I pushed her off the sidewalk, threw sand in her hair. And thereby launched the most successful career as a beach-boy since Erik Estrada.

Actually, it took me somewhat longer to learn to meet girls. A lot longer. Say, four years at college and three years at Missiles and Space. Then I got laid off by the company and got the chance to put what I'd learned into practice.

Lesson 1 (Nancy's rule): *If you want a date with a girl, the first thing you must do is to ask her.* I asked the girl behind the counter, judging her a nine. She was Italian or a little Italian, full breasted on a small frame, long hair, lots of makeup, long eyelashes, long, sharp fingernails. "I like your hands," I said. "Tell me your name. Your name, your phone number. Give me a chance to call you when I know something's happening."

(See the way I come on? Strong, forceful, in control.)

"Something's happening?" she replied, her voice like honey on macadamia-nut pancakes. She was alive and paying attention to me. (How do these things work? Why is meeting people such an art?)

"I'd take you to coffee," I babbled, "If I knew where they served the best coffee in Honolulu. I'd take you to Lums and buy you a beer if it were two in the morning and we were on the mainland. But I... I'm Haole here."

Lesson 2: *Keep Talking.* It's not what you say that's important. It's that you pay attention to the one you're with."

My girl——the Italian, was paying attention to me. (Or was she cracking up, laughing.) Maybe she thought I was some kind of nut. Maybe she thought I was the greatest. The important thing was she was talking to me, no longer a fantasy, thinking it over.

"Haole. You're new." she said thoughtfully. (She knew I knew she was thinking it over. She looked me up and down while she thought.)

"Haole, there's a place a lot of people go to. Called the Green Lobster. Beer, pretzels, everybody sings along with the band. If you like that sort of thing?"

The sort of thing I like is a rich full mouth, long sharp fingernails, and a set of big, full breasts, preferably pointing in different directions. Beer parlors are O.K. for celebrating after an exam or a liftoff. But they're noisy, the bandsmen are raunchy, the sawdust is there just to cover the beer the waiters spill.

Be positive: that's Lesson Three. Girls like men that know how to have fun. Beer parlors are pretty neat places. So much is going on, you don't need to make conversation, just sit and wink and drink.

Afterward, she took me home like all good island girls in the storybooks. She stayed home from work the next couple of days with a 'cold', and when we weren't making love in her apartment, we'd be parked somewhere high above the surf making love in her car. If we weren't doing it in the back seat, her long perfect fingers would be inside my fly, tugging and caressing, getting me ready for action again.

Girl liked variety; she liked me in her mouth, and she liked me between her legs. Sometimes, we'd do both, alternating back and forth until I no longer had any control and came violently inside her or against the seat. But seven days of lovemaking, seven days and six nights, were all my Hawaiian tour allowed. "Girl," I said, "I've got to get back on the tour."

"You told me you were new," she said, sounding betrayed, "You said you came here to look for a job and settle down."

I explained about the tour, the seven days and six nights in Hawaii by the grace of InterCosmopolitan and their low, low all-inclusive fares. I told her about the bus that took you around to all the sights, and then brought you back to your hotel again.

"You kind of got off the tour," she said. She no longer sounded disappointed and unwilling to understand. And she let her fingers do the walking down my thigh.

I had gotten off the tour... at the very first opportunity. The let downs began in the Los Angeles airport with each glimpse of my gaggle of fellow tourists. A collection of turkeys and turkeyettes from the first spinster schoolteacher to the final candidate for 'Miss Mouse'. The Bon Voyage party —another of the fabled attractions of the 'Club InterCosmopolitan,' sagged rather than sparkled.

The 'Club' was a gimmick. A five-buck membership included in the tour price allowed InterCosmo to book us all at a reduced rate —at least, that's what the salesperson told me. Whatever, it wasn't such a bad deal for them or me. And a Hawaiian tour had seemed a hell of a good way to pass the time till I got another job. (O.K., so there isn't any prospect of my getting another job until we have our next war.)

Lesson 4: *If it looks too good to be true, grab it!*

My island girl believed in coming before going. I don't know why I left her. I was in the twenty-fourth week of my unemployment insurance, the next to last week. I would have been better off to stay in Hawaii, forget the unemployment checks and start over. Instead, I took the next bus to the airport, alone. I had a bag I'd kept with me, and the hope that, somehow, InterCosmo had been shifting the rest of my luggage from hotel to hotel along with the tour.

Lesson 5: *Never pack more than you can carry with you.*

Mr. Drake, aging lavender director of InterCosmo, was not there to greet me at the ticket counter. Instead, a brusque voice, "I'm sorry Sir. You'll have to talk with the passenger agent."

The passenger agent smiled a lot. "We aren't able to accept these tickets, I'm afraid (smile). Your agency was in error in selling them. You may be able to get your money back (smile) when you return to the Mainland. Though I hear they've gone out of business (smile)."

"What about the tour! the hotels?! my luggage? What about the other people on the tour?"

"I suggest you do as they did several days ago, Sir. Buy a ticket for your return flight and arrange for alternate accommodations till then (no smile)."

"How! with my unemployment check?!"

"That's really not the airline's affair. Is it, Sir? If you wish, we might..." he began. But I'd stalked away.

Two of the mice from the tour were waving to me from across the airport terminal. The brown-haired one was a clinger, the touch of her twig-like fingers a prelude to a nasal monotone. She clung now to the hairy arm of her constant companion, a dark-haired plump Sicilian girl with her own form of speech impediment. Were they schoolteachers? librarians? social workers? They'd tried to sit next to me, to Grandfather Barnes, even to Mr. Drake, a determined homosexual if ever there was one. "Bon voyage", I'd wished them as I fled the tours, and now...

"We're all together again," said Miss Mouse.

"You're back!" black-hair brayed.

"What about our tickets?" I raged.

"Oh, we're going to stay another two weeks," mousy brown giggled. "We're...," she mumbled, "Would you like to ...?"

"NO!" I shouted, already strides away. "No," I said to myself, "no, no, no."

Back to the airport bus. Fare 45 cents. Cash on hand, 47 cents. Resources: one travelers check for twenty dollars; one poncho —army surplus; one tote bag containing razor, bathing suit, condoms. And waiting in the heart of the San Fernando Valley, just outside beautiful downtown Burbank, three unemployment checks that had to be signed and countersigned in person.

132

Lesson 6: You can't pick it up where you left off. You can't rekindle an old flame. You... But I was too angry to put my feelings into words. I stood outside her window, waiting in the rain. My Island beauty was inside, warm and comfortable. She had company. The cries coming from her window were familiar. But someone else was inside her.

I undressed on her porch and hung my suit on a hanger that had held my poncho. I hung my last dress shirt under the suit. I put on my bathing suit, my Primo sports shirt, and the poncho. I left the suit and the dress shirt along with a note —"Please have this suit cleaned and pressed by Friday." Then I walked away.

It took a lot of walking. It was morning before I reached the coast, noon before a series of rides brought me to the cliffs at the edge of the Waipio valley. The valley was a deep cleft in the volcanic rock, "a descent into the primitive," read the guidebook. I remember the view at the valley's edge, vividly. It is still as real to me as the long nights of rain when I lay huddled in my poncho and the flood that drove me out of the valley.

Far, far below was a narrow alluvial plane, the river running to the sea, and the black volcanic beach. A jeep trail marked '4 wheel vehicles only' wound down the cliff. Across the beach, a second great slab of stone sealed off the valley. Both cliffs reached far out into the sea so there was no escape.

The jeep trail disappeared into a low cloud. Sometimes as I walked, I could see across the valley —the lush rain forests, like hanging gardens, the silver green of the Koa, the dark green of the Maile tree. And sometimes, I could see nothing at all in the mists. As I rounded an outside curve, the wind tore at my shoulders. Far below were the sea sands, jet-black beneath the surf. Far off in the stiff shore breeze, the cold waves dashed on the rocks, a sound like wooden ships breaking and the screams of children. The mist was cold and damp; it swallowed the sounds and light and everything I remembered.

I could see only the trail itself, the small signs of animal life, the ferns and the vines that led the way back up the hillside. The pig persimmons, a type of shrub, bore a small green fruit about the size of my fist. They were

133

tasty, but the juicy pulp was filled with seeds. The same seeds lay untouched in the lumps of animal feces that dotted the trail.

Guava grew there too, both sweet and sour, and papaya, and granddaddy cocoanuts. I have eaten the green cocoanuts they sell at Waikiki, with the juice still spicy and effervescent, and the stale cocoanuts they sell in the grocery stores on the mainland, but these granddaddies were a third, entirely different fruit. Ripe of its own accord, inside the shriveled husk juice and pulp had merged into a gigantic ball of toasted cocoanut candy.

Within the valley, the trail paralleled the river, a broad, deep stream that divided the valley in two. The river had numerous branches that surrounded and filled the farm patches of taro and rice. A farmhouse could occasionally be glimpsed in the mist. Each time the trail split, I chose the branch that kept me furthest away from them.

A dog had followed me down through the mists. He raced in and out of the underbrush, though he preferred a trailing position about ten paces behind me. Whenever I looked back, the dog was crouched, head up, as if to say "Can I come?" And I always jerked my head forward to reply, "Onward, man and dog."

The river was not impassible, as I'd imagined in my first glimpse from the cliffs above. It grew shallower as it branched and subdivided. I took off my shoes and waded each time the trail crossed or merged with a stream. After awhile I discarded my trousers. They were too wet and too encumbering.

By evening, I found a relatively dry patch of ground on which to camp, and proceeded to gather a small supply of guava and granddaddy cocoanuts. Nightfall was abrupt and terrifying, ending in an all-enveloping darkness. Although it was only seven or eight in the evening, I lay down on the ground in my poncho and tried to sleep. I dreamt of parking in the hills above Los Angeles, someone next to me on the seat, and the lights of the city below. I slept in fits and starts, waking each time to that terrifying blackness. (My dog slept near me in the darkness. I could hear him breathing, but I could not see him.)

The next day it began to rain, a light rain that continued throughout the day. I gathered palm fronds and built a lean-to against the tree. Not solid enough to keep the rain out, but enough to break its fall.

On the fourth day, while I was preparing my evening meal —boiled freshwater shrimp and papaya —a horse wandered into my clearing. Dog ran to the horse and walked around him sniffing. The horse ignored Dog. Dog ran to me to complain. Then, we heard the horse's owner call to him.

A boy walked into the clearing dragging a huge palm frond behind him. The boy was about eighteen years of age. He was nude. Two more young men followed him. They each wore a loincloth. "Hi," they said, one after the other.

I tried to look at them and not to look at them. They eyed my shrimp. "We eat only vegetables," one said, "Papaya, we eat only papaya. Ten or twelve a day." His belly was huge, distended. It hung over his loincloth. All three had huge, distended bellies. "Sometimes, we eat cocoanut," he said wistfully.

I gave them one of my cocoanuts.

"I've been here almost one year," said the talkative one. "They've been here almost two. We're hiding from the draft." He paused, lifted his loincloth, and urinated against the tree.

"I sleep in my poncho," I said. There was a long silence. "You should eat shrimp," I continued, "high protein." There was another long silence. I was conscious I hadn't eaten my evening meal and that soon it would be dark.

Then they were gone. Lightning streaked across the sky followed by the distance sound of thunder. Night came. I slept. An hour or so later, the rain, no more than a light drizzle at first, forced its way beneath my poncho and began to pelt my forehead. I could hear the water dropping through the branches, a "swish, gurgle, gurgle" from a nearby stream. Reaching out a hand for support, I felt it plunge beneath the rising water.

All at once, I longed for the comfort of a parked car, the glimmer of a light. The wind blew the rain through an opening in the roof. My hut collapsed; the sodden branches fell across me. Soon I was sleeping in the stream.

Absolutely black. Not a glow, not a glimmer, like the inside of a cave where bats go to hide during the day. I couldn't see the trail or even guess where it began. And I was lying in the water! I had to escape and had no way of escaping.

I spent the night standing, sleeping against the tree, and, of course, feeling generally sorry for myself. In the morning Dog was gone. The trail, too, had vanished. I was ready to go home and set out wading along the streambed. Where I could, I climbed the hillside to keep out of the water. Only after it was too late did I realize my mistake. I was on the wrong side of the valley.

Far off there was an intermittent rumble, the sound of the waves striking the beach. Behind was the stream. Ahead, huge boulders barred my path to the beach. Tossed carelessly aside by an ancient volcano, each rock was a separate journey for me. Up, find a foothold, down. Never straight ahead.

The rocks grew smaller as I drew further from the valley, and closer to the ocean. I could step with care from one to another. The shore wind grew in intensity as I walked, whipping the poncho over my head like an inside-out umbrella, forcing me to walk doubled over.

I came to where I could see the ocean. No beach here, no clean white sand. Waves fell directly on the stones, hissing as they sought to escape back to sea. Gray-green breakers rose a hundred yards or more from shore, built, crested, and smashed against the rocks.

Turning my back on the shore to confront the river, I saw that the main stream, forty yards wide and swollen by the rains, had drawn almost level with its banks. If I slipped while crossing, I would be swept out into the surf where the dull thud of the cleansing breakers repeatedly pounded the rocks. Afraid, I turned and walked back into the valley where I'd spent the night, where the stream was narrower and the waters calmer.

I walked until I could no longer see the sea, to where the sound of water dripping through the trees could compete with the hissing of the waves. The current was strong here, too, but I was just able to keep my balance. The water rose from my waist to my chest. It covered the shoes that I had slung around my neck. I stood on tiptoe for a moment fighting against the current. Then I had crossed the halfway point and the water began to go down again. On the far shore, I found Dog.

The climb out of the Valley was fatiguing, almost monotonous. Dog barked at my heels for most of the climb, barring her teeth. Near the top, I thought mainly about my hunger.

More walking and a couple of lucky rides. I retrieved my suit —it hadn't been cleaned or pressed and no one answered my knock-—and headed for tourist land. My plan was to sleep in a hotel lobby, but the wrinkles in my suit soon gave me away. The hotel detectives rousted me.

"On your feet."

"I'm waiting for the airport limousine."

"Wait outside."

I moved a dozen times that night. During the day, I got by on the beach, sleeping, gazing at an ocean of browning flesh, winking at the broads, waiting to be discovered.

I wanted to be part of something. And, finally, Hawaii welcomed me. The banners were all over the Hotel district: "Welcome American Society of Systems Programmers and Computer Personnel." ASSPCP, that was me! A computer person for over four years, and an ASSPCP member. (At least, I had been when Missiles and Space was paying my way.)

"Hi, Jim. Jim?" a voice called out behind me.

Someone was calling my name.

It had started! I was just inside the door of the conference and I was practically back at work again!

I turned and the face and voice came together in my mind. "Hi Al, long time. . . ," I began.

"Jimbo. Good to see you. Kubreck spring for your trip to Hawaii? I should have joined you people. I'm a Programmer IV now though."

(Kubreck? Spring for a trip? Oh, yeah. Kubreck had all this talk about starting a consulting firm. I was going to be a vice-president. I'd even tried to recruit Al back then. But Al had stayed with Missiles and Space wanting the security. Smart move. Hey, maybe Al would recruit me! Maybe someone would.)

"Hi, Jim."

Someone else saying hello. I knew the face, I couldn't remember the name. I answered "Hi," but the face didn't stop to chat. I know the name that goes with this next face: Dr. Barnes, my old section chief at M&S. He'd said he'd hire me back as soon as there was an opening. "Hi, Doc."

Not even a "Hi" out of him in return, just a nod as he walks by.

"Don't worry about Dr. Barnes," Al said, "he's got a lot on his mind. You'll be seeing him at the banquet. All the gang will be getting together afterwards. You, too. Hey. Where you staying?"

"I'm... not registered yet."

"You gotta get registered." Al said.

We were in the registration line. The girl said, "Name?"

"Smith. James S. Smith."

She typed two lines and handed me a plastic badge that read "Aloha, Hawaii welcomes you, ASSPCP 13th Annual, James S. Smith," along with a program guide and a map of Honolulu.

"Pre-registered?", the girl asked.

"Uh... Yeah."

138

"Can't find your name." The girl smiled. "This whole thing is so screwed up anyway. Doesn't matter. Dammed computers. Find your hotel OK?"

"They, uh, don't seem to have a record of my reservation."

"Hey Jimbo," Al put in, "I thought you were staying here."

"Shut up, Al," I prayed, hoping the sweat didn't show on my forehead, "Shut up."

The girl didn't seem to have heard him. Thank God. She was gorgeous, lovely, dark, Hawaiian, not Italian. She caught me looking. "Take this voucher over to the registration desk," she said. "You can straighten the whole thing out with InterCosmopolitan when you get back to Los Angeles."

I choked. "InterCosmo is handling the convention!"

"That's my employer. We handle conventions, tours and travel reservations. Do I look like a computer person?

"Have a nice time in Hawaii, Mr. Smith." A smile and she went on to the next registrant, "Name?"

As in a dream, I walked across the lobby, presented the voucher the girl had given me, signed the hotel register, and, fending off the tip-hungry bellmen, went to my room. I sat on the edge of the bed for a long time, staring at the view that $185 a day bought in Waikiki —the view, the color TV, and a set of luggage marked H. Krumball.

H (for Henry) was my size. H himself didn't show up for two more days. (Where had he been?) When he did, he accepted my apologies with an alcoholic's good grace and took back all his suits. For those two, three days I had a ball —banquets, luncheons, long rap sessions at the pool. Girls in and out of every room. Women I had known before, women whose names I didn't catch. Guys who bought me drinks, guys who talked around the possibility—just the possibility—of a job back in L.A.

So I finally got back on the tour. And guess who else was there? Miss Mouse and her pudgy, dark friend. They weren't schoolteachers after all, but programmers like me! I gave them a big hello——like old friends from school, and avoided them whenever I could. It wasn't always easy. They had the same book of tickets I did, the little book InterCosmopolitan had left for Henry and me. The book contained tickets for banquets (I left after the meal, before the opening speeches), a lunch with fashion show for the ladies (I stayed for the ladies), even a guided tour of Diamond Head.

Mousy Brown sat next to the strapping beach boy who drove the bus. I sat in the back with Dolly Ginsburg, (born Smith). Dolly just had to have the greatest pair of nose cones in the missiles and space business. She was also the life of every party until Al Ginsburg grounded her. (In private and afterwards, Dolly could be a bore. "I love Al. I should have stayed with Tom. Tom's no good. Al is so good to me. I don't know what to do..." and so on in a heavy nasal accent.) In public, with a little bit of booze inside here, Dolly was fun, fun, fun.

She had all of us in the back of the bus in stitches. I don't know whether those people knew each other when they got on the bus, but they sure knew each other when they got off. Everyone was getting up and changing seats and yelling back and forth and singing. You could hardly hear the PA system with its "Kamenhahemaha Day celebrates the coronation . . . " But the tour guide turned out to be a tremendous sport, and he led us all into Diamond Head singing at the top of our lungs.

So, it's all a memory. A nice memory, like that night in the Green Lobster, with no need to do anything but be. We're at Diamond Head, a bunch of crazies running around the parking lot. Giggling, too drunk to sing, passing a hurricane glass filled with rum. Then we're back at the hotel in Waikiki and they're taking down the exhibits.

The registration tables have been dismantled, the welcome signs replaced by something in Japanese. People are talking about the planes they're going to catch, shouting "Good-bye, see you in Boston." A few people are coming up to me, the ones I'd sort of thought I'd remembered, saying "Hi, I thought it was you," and then they are gone too.

"See you in Boston." Even Henry showed up in time to pick up his bags and take back his suits again. (Where were you Henry? Where are you now?)

Two p.m., check out time. I hung around in the lobby until six when the hotel detectives started to give me the eye. No way to blend, no one I could blend with. Unless... Across the lobby are my old friends, mousy brown and pudgy black. Pudgy has spent the intervening week growing a three-inch hair on her chin. She is still the cuter of the two. Mousy brown has a face like an axe head, pure New England, and a spare little body that says I want to be loved, lend me the equipment.

Mousy drags her friend forward, gives me the arm too, clinging. Black hair is the one that speaks, crooning the lyrics from a new reggae tune:

"In the Aquarian age, we understand,

Sometime, the woman, she ask the man."

We go to their room. They order me dinner. We spend the rest of the evening fucking. I fuck them on every piece of furniture in the room, on the rug, on the floor, in the bathtub. They know how to use their hands to arouse real passion. And they come conveniently often. I release one, top the other, keep moving. Pause, thrust, suck, keep stiff.

They screamed the whole time, pleasure mostly. They begged me to stop and they begged me to keep doing it. Not endearments, these were orders. I slept when they slept. When they woke I was made to be ready for them.

The idea came to me in the night, just the core of an idea, not the whole thing, that maybe this was the way it was supposed to be for me. The three of us together back in L.A. sharing an apartment. All of us working, with me taking turns to please them.

In the morning, after they had packed, the brown-haired one handed me two twenty-dollar bills without looking up at me, and I knew it wasn't going to be like that.

I can't tell if this is a true story or just fiction," I said to my Dad.

"What's the difference?"

"Well, that last story of yours I read, the one about the rock concert, seemed pretty autobiographical to me."

He shrugged. "I never said it was."

"Is this one? Dad! Did you go to Hawaii?"

"Yes. Right before I met your mother. And when I came back to the mainland, I drove to Pasadena in time to park and see the Rose Bowl Parade."

We were making progress; "Dad! Were you ever a beach boy?"

"No comment."

"Did you sneak into a convention?"

"Not in Hawaii, a couple of years later, when I was in Lake Placid. And there wasn't a Henry, but Jim Thompson did let me sleep on his couch in the Hilton once when there were no rooms available."

"Those two girls in the hotel. Were they real?"

"There's been a lot of girls. Remember that when some guy tells you you're the only girl in his life."

"Thanks. I'm not an idiot, Dad. Were you ever on a guided tour? Was there a Mr. Drake?"

"Drake was later, when your mother and I lived in Maryland."

"So parts of the story are true, right? And parts are fiction. You just mixed them together?" But he merely smiled, enigmatically, and kissed me, or rather, tried to kiss me on the forehead. Why did I draw back? And later, he looked so hurt. I want him to hug me; I don't want him to hug me. What is the matter with me?

142

We used to have a large house, and a lot of land when we lived in Michigan, a large yard when we lived in Georgia. Maryland, Michigan, Georgia, California, I'd start to make friends in school, to bring them home, to have them invite me to their homes, and then we'd move again.

"Dad, did you have trouble keeping a job?" And my Dad, still hurt by my drawing away from his caress, did not answer. I babbled on, "I mean in these two stories, both times, you talk about being out of a job."

"I've been between jobs a couple of times."

"Do you have tenure, now?"

"No, I don't"

"So you could be unemployed again?'

"Where's this going, honey?"

"Well, I was thinking about myself. I mean, here I'm getting my high school diploma and I'm pretty sure I'm going to be able to get a teacher's credential too, but what if there isn't a job for me when I get through?"

"I guess you put an ad in the paper."

"What?"

"Young attractive girl, 19, looking for love compassion..." He stopped abruptly; he must have seen the hurt look on my face. "I don't know what to tell you, honey. I don't even know what to tell myself. The jobs come, the jobs go. In the end, you're probably going to get by with a little help from your friends."

"Like the gang I used to live with."

"You can do better than that."

She burst into tears. I held her and I hugged her.

143

19.   Seven Days in May

May 13: Executive Vice President Earl Cheit says the University will not move in the middle of the night to destroy the People's Park.

May 15, 3am (the middle of the night):   200 Berkeley and campus police move in and surround People's Park. Alameda County Sheriff deputies fire at will. Two on rooftops felled by buckshot.

May 16: People rally. March on park. National Guard called out.

May 18: National Guard blockades downtown Berkeley forestalling march and vigil. People open People's Park #2 at Grove and Hearst.

May 19: Rally in Sproul Plaza broken up by National Guard with bayonets.

May 20: Berkeley City Council in emergency session resolves to ask grand jury to investigate violence used to suppress the "violence." Tear gas dropped on campus by Army helicopters.

May 21, 10pm: South campus open to all traffic. Nightlife reappears on Telegraph Avenue

Chapter 20. Taking Coup

"Did you ever have any adventures of your own, Uncle Pete? I mean an adventure which didn't involve my dad?"

"Does the Peace Corp count?   I was in India for two years."

"Wow, you mean like when the Beetles were in India with the Maharishi."

"Oh, no. Years before that. I joined the Peace Corps about the time of Kennedy's speech. You know," he lowered his voice, pretending it was coming out of the T.V., " 'Ask not what your country can do for you...'"

I shook my head. "No, Uncle Pete. It's got to be in the sixties."

"Well that was in the sixties. Kennedy was in the sixties."

"Bobby Kennedy?"

"No, Jack Kennedy. The President. There was a lot of sixties."

"Kennedy was too long ago. I mean later, when you were in Berkeley and everything was happening."

"You know, Dina, there was life before the Beetles."

I gave him a look.

"O.K. A Berkeley adventure. I was living on Dwight Way just below Shattuck—you remember, you stayed there with me once when you came out to visit?"

I nodded, although to be honest, I didn't remember where his apartment was. I was only five or six years old at the time.

"Well, anyway, I decided to go out for breakfast one morning—maybe because you weren't there to fix us corn flakes with bananas. There was this restaurant on Shattuck I always went to. They made a pretty big omelet for the money and the coffee was good. All the refills you wanted.

"It was one of those really fine Fall mornings. None of this wait-till-eleven-for-the-fog-to-lift we usually have in Berkeley the other nine months of the year. The sky was already clear and blue, and I'd be looking at the sun just as soon as it rose high enough to clear the Oakland Hills. Early enough, there's nobody on the street window shopping and late enough, there's nobody going to work. The only one in sight was this tall bearded guy leaning against the front of the restaurant. A typical Berkeley street person, he looked like he'd slept in his clothes.

"I like to read while I'm eating. So before I walked into the restaurant, I stopped to buy a paper. I was just taking it out of the rack, when this guy comes up and says don't shut the rack, give him one too. Of course, I shut the rack right away. I mean if people don't pay for papers, they'll have to raise the price for the people who do pay.

"Well this guy gets mad and all of a sudden he's swinging and hitting me."

"Did you win the fight?"

"Yeah. After we'd traded punches for a few minutes. But he chipped one of my teeth first." Pete opened his mouth to show me where one of his incisors had a slight wedge missing from its corner.

"My dad says you usually try to avoid fights."

"Hey. Not if somebody hits me first."

"I understand. You know it's funny about you and my dad being Quakers. I mean you're supposed to be pacifists and you're always getting into fights."

"Hey, it was just this one time. Your dad is the one to watch out for."

"Why is my dad a Quaker? He doesn't seem like a pacifist to me. He loses his temper so easily."

"And he knows that he's wrong. He's been trying to change himself for years. Quakerism is just another way of getting at his anger and channeling it into something useful."

This sounded an awful lot like a lecture to me. "I'm not sure if the story you told me is really an adventure," I said.

"No," he said, grinning, Uncle Pete always grins when he is nervous, "But it shows you what life in Berkeley was like as we started to move out of the sixties.

Suddenly, Pete stopped talking and his brow went vacant the way it does when he is discovering a theorem or something. When he spoke, it was slowly, seriously, as if he were not just telling an anecdote but were actually there, reliving the experience.

"I've thought of an adventure and it's authentic '60s Berkeley, too. You'll like this one. You may have read about all the protests in the sixties?

"Well, one time, things got so out of hand in Berkeley—it was mostly the untrained Alameda County Sheriff's deputies that got out of hand; the Blue Meanies we called them—that they had to call in the National Guard.

"Everyday for a week, there were helicopters buzzing the campus and laying down a stream of tear gas. Berkeley was like one of those towns you read about in Europe, students at the barricades, National Guardsman and police everywhere. Security at the University was even tighter. If you wanted to return a book to the library, you had to

147

go through five lines of police. I forget the order, but you had the Sheriff's department, the Berkeley City Police, the campus police reinforced by the state highway patrol on the outside of campus, then the National Guard and finally the campus police again when you got close to the library building.

"Now, I had library books to return, but more important I also needed a library book that I'd left in my office. The problem was how to keep the trigger-happy policemen from gunning me down while I was going for the book.

"It was bad enough just going to class in those days. You'd be walking between buildings, maybe keeping your eye on some girl a few steps ahead, wondering what you could say to her to open up a conversation, when, all of a sudden, you'd hear the helicopters and you'd smell the tear gas, and, whoosh, you'd be running just as fast as you could trying to get away. All this, and it would still be twenty minutes or so before you'd come in range of the bullhorns telling the crowds to disperse on some completely different part of campus.

"Once, I had to hold my head in Strawberry Creek for what seemed like an hour, trying to wash the poison out of my eyes and staying close to the ground so that I wouldn't get any more in my lungs."

"Was my dad. . .?"

"No. Your dad was long gone and working for a living; you wanted a story about me and this is it.

"So anyway. It's Sunday. One of those glorious Sundays when I could sleep in and did, your father not being around. I woke up finally and decided after breakfasting on a bowl of instant Quaker oatmeal, the apple-cinnamon flavor, that what I really wanted to do was to finish working on the theorem I'd been working on the previous night. Well, I looked over the books that were spread across my kitchen table and remember that the book I need, and the reason I stopped

148

working around three or four in the morning, is not there but in my office on campus.

"My office is in one of those Quonset huts they put up in the forties after the second world war to house the overflow of students that came back to study under the G.I. bill. Those wooden temporary buildings may be the second oldest buildings on campus after Founder's Hall. They're right in the center of campus, just north of the library. I can see the route in my mind. From where I was living then, I could bike over and back in fifteen minutes. I could walk there in the same amount of time. But what about the State of Emergency? Could I get through the police lines to my office?

"The curfew is lifted at eight in the morning, so it's safe to go out into the street, but if I try to walk toward campus, I know the police or the National Guard are going to turn me away. I walk along Oxford anyway and two armored personnel carriers pass me going in the same direction. The corner of Oxford and Berkeley has got two police cars parked in the intersection, so I duck back up a side street—it's a little out of my way, because now I've got to walk a long way up a hill and a long way down a hill to get to where I could have got to ordinarily by walking a curve around the bottom. I came down finally on one side of Berkeley Avenue with the north side of Campus ahead of me on the opposite side. All I've got to do to get to the University is to run across the street and into the bushes without anybody seeing me. And I do it quickly, before I say to myself, this is the sort of thing that Phil would do, it's not the sort of thing that I would do."

"Is that really true?" I asked Pete, "That my dad's the sort of guy that gets into trouble while you just sort of go along?"

"Yes and no. I'm more conservative than your father, but I can get just as angry when people back me into a corner or try to get me to do something I don't want to do. Maybe, it's that when your dad is around we do so many crazy things together that I use up my own quota. Then, when he's gone, I crave excitement again, which is why

149

I found myself crouching in the bushes that Sunday with the street on one side of me and the campus access road on the other.

"I walk east on campus, staying in the line of bushes. East, by the way, means straight uphill. I stay on the campus side most of the time, unless I hear a car, then I duck back in the bushes, no thorns most of the time. Once, I'm hiding in the bushes from a campus patrol car, when a city police car pulls to a halt on the street near me and parks there—God, my heart is beating—while the officers roust some poor student who's just walking along the street or trying to go to his office like I am. They don't book him or anything, just order him to go back to his house and get away from campus, so I figure that's the worst that can happen to me, unless I run into one of the Blue Meanies or a trigger-happy National Guardsman!

"The line of bushes come to an end, finally, and then it's a question of skipping across from concrete island to concrete island until I can find shelter again up against a building or behind a tree, what few are left with all the construction going on. Just to be on the safe side, I check the doors on a couple of the buildings to see if I can maybe duck in if I get trapped; but they're all locked. So, I'm back to playing Puss-in-the-Corner with real bullets whenever I'm in the open.

"Incidentally, I got my excitement quota for the year that morning. I get to a hill overlooking the temporary buildings where my office is and what do I see on the lawn next to them: Tents. Army tents. Who is inside the tents? I can't see. No one is moving around on the ground near the tents, but this doesn't mean there is no one inside them. There are big ditches everywhere—it's part of the construction they're doing on campus before the trouble started—and any running I do is not going to be in a straight line. I just hope whoever is in the tents won't shoot if they do see me. Not until they've at least shouted a warning.

"A campus police car goes by on the road between the library and the temporary buildings. I can hear someone talking over the police radio even if I can't make out the words. I wait for the car to pass, and try to guess how many minutes it's going to be before the next one comes along or somebody comes back to the tents. Then, I'm running down the hill like a mad fool, faster than I should be running over rough ground, especially since when I get to the building door, I've got to fumble with my key and get the wrong one and get the right one in the lock only just as I begin hearing a voice coming out of a police radio. It's a walkie-talkie. The voice gets louder and two sheriff's deputies walk by. But by that time, I'm crouched on the floor of the temporary building, my back to the wooden door, puffing away. They walk on; they don't see me.

"My second-floor office has a great view of nothing. The window opening encompasses a portion of the access road and the lane leading to the library and the after-hours book return slot. I can just make out a portion of the tents on the lawn below, if, that is, I flatten myself against the wall on the far side of the window. I figure the best thing to do is to stay well back in the room while I'm looking out so that nobody will see me. Incredibly, while I'm watching, two different people come and drop books in the library return slot. It's that kind of Sunday or else taking coup must be the new in thing on the campus. Once, I thought I could smell tear gas, and once I think I can hear shots. I read in Monday's newspaper that there were shots fired that day, though not on campus, but in one of the buildings on the south side. They actually shot and killed a student, James Rector, who'd been watching them from a rooftop.

"Originally, I thought I'd sit down and work on the theorem at my desk for an hour or so in case I needed another book from my office, but I panicked, almost the moment I sat down. Couldn't have been more than five minutes and I was outside again—what else should I have done, spend the night in my office? I walked back to my apartment along almost exactly the route I had come."

"But you had the book."

"No." A guilty look spread across Pete's face, although it was now almost two decades since he had snuck onto campus through the police lines. "I'd started reading at my desk, and, then, when I smelled the tear gas, I just got up and walked out. I was halfway back to my apartment before I even thought about the book."

21. Don't give a Damn 'bout Viet Nam

The second midterm had come and gone and I'd got all A's. And one B that I hadn't told my father about. I'd gotten confused about one part of the test. I went to see the instructor during his office hours; he explained the concept to me and I'm sure I understand it now. I asked him if he'd give me another set of exercises so I could check out my understanding. He looked surprised, but gave me another book to use. So you see, I don't need to tell my dad.

Dear Aimai: Hi. My name is Dave.

I was reading Barb, when I came across your ad. I usually don't believe in this kind of stuff, but I just couldn't get your ad out of my mind. For some reason I believe that you are a very beautiful person and perhaps you are lonely like me?

Well, guess I'd better start telling you about me. I'm in the Marine Corps. I'm a corporal, I was in Viet Nam last year. I'm stationed at MCRD, 3rd Bat, 3rd RTR. I'm a drill instructor. My full name is Thomas Arthur Roberts.

I don't know where the Dave came from, although my mother tells me that when I was little I used to drink left over beer out of the bottles. So that everybody started calling me Dave. (I know it doesn't make much sense.)

I was born in a small town called Azalea in Ohio. You've never heard of it, I bet. Most people out here haven't. I was born in the Azalea Hospital on the 10th of June. I don't know how much I weighed or what time it was when I caught my first wind. Any way I guess that's not important.

I guess you want to know what some of my likes and dislikes are.

Well, to start with, I like women very much. I believe that a true man is only a half a man without a woman. What do you think?

I like sports of all kinds. The two I like best are football and basketball. What's your favorite sports?

Now to get down to the real nitty ritty. Aimai, I can love if you can love. I want someone to want, need, and love me.

Aimai, maybe you might know the feeling too, huh?

I've been in love before and it was beautiful. She . . .

"You didn't finish reading that letter," my father said. Apparently, he wasn't one hundred percent into his work the way I thought he was.

"I may read it later," I said. "I'm reading this stuff for fun. It's not a research project."

D p cl/#Łxyh#ehhq#lq#oryh#ehiruh#dqg#lw#dv#ehdxwlixd#Vkh#oryhg#
p h#dqg#hhghg#h#dqg#l#kh#dp h#iru#khu#Nkhq#zkhq#l#fdp h#
kqw#kh#hxylfh#p |#krdh#urg#fdp h#dsduw#Vkh#hniw#h#ru#
dqrwkhu#Hyhu|#dqfh#khq#Łxyh#ehhq#orrnlqj#iru#oryh1#Vxuh/#
wkh#whuh#lp hv#zkhq#l#krxjkw#l#rxqg#lw#exw#dwbddz d|#zhqw#
vrxu1#

##P d|eh#zh#rq#wdoo#lq#oryh1#Zh#txw#p ljkw#ehfrp h#jrrg#
iulhqgv1##jhhg#vrp herg|#D p d|#vr#sdovh#zulwh#p h#edfn/#R N 1##

##Wkdqnv#Vzhhw|#

##Gdyh#

Dad? How can you tell if somebody is telling you the truth? Like in these letters: Is it a line? Do they write the same thing to every girl? Or are they sincere?"

"You can only tell the truth by people's actions, by what they do, not by what they say. When I'm face to face with someone, I think I can tell if they are telling me the truth. I think I can. I always knew when you were lying and you were the least truthful of my children. It's in the eyes. In your case, you even stick your tongue in your cheek when you lie. But what we're talking about here is a guy writing to a girl, and what is written will always be both fake and real. The feeling is real: I mean the guy who wrote it, who really wrote it—in case they're having somebody else ghost the letter for them—he had those feelings. But whether he had those feelings for you or for some other girl, you'll have no way of telling until you see him face to face, and even then you won't be sure until you've seen what he does the next day and the day after that.

"One thing you can discern from a letter is those that feel from those who live in their heads separate from their feelings. You're still better off with someone who can laugh and cry even if their feelings may not be directed toward you at first."

"Like you, Dad?" I said, bitterly. I don't know why I was so bitter; maybe, I still expected more from him; maybe, I was mad because of the unkind thing he'd said about me. It may have been true once.

"They say girls always marry men like their fathers," he concluded smugly. So smug. I guess I'm going to have a smug husband.

> Aimai: I hope I'm not too late in
> replying. I was med-evacuated from Nam to
> Japan with hepatitis (a very good sham)
> and I happened to meet a guy who had an
> issue of Barb and I snatched it from him,

When I saw the ad I was really turned on and happy.

I hope this letter doesn't sound strange, but I've been here for seven months and my mind is not functioning as well as when I came. I left Japan to return to Nam on January 15th and I am back in the big hole. The Vietnamese people are making too much money from this war to want it to end. They work for us during the day as barbers, housegirls, and hired help and at nite they work for the VC in various jobs. The kids really make a mint selling grass (that's okay) but the C.I.D. (army fuzz) is trying to blow that. A lot of guys send kilos home (a kilo here is $25 at the most) with various methods.

I'll get out of the army when I leave Nam which is a real pleasure. These lifers (career army) really fuck with guys who hate the army. They are always bugging us about getting haircuts and trimming mustaches. That really pisses me off because Nam is bad enough without some high ranking fool lifer rapping about unnecessary things.

I'm luckily not in the infantry. I'm in supply and stay mostly at our base camp. I used to drive a gasoline truck throu Saigon to our units down there.

I leave Viet Nam to return to the world at the end of June. We are still waiting for the TET offensive. Tet is the Vietnamese lunar New Year and the VC usually try a big surge during the celebration.

I sure wish I knew what was happening in the world. When I get back I want to be with someone before i go home and rehumanize myself and catch up with what is happening. We lived in Joliet and also in Dallas TX which I hate to claim. Dallas is a good market for bands (I was lead singer in one when I got drafted) but otherwise it sucks. My parents live there with my brothers and sisters.

This is a kinda cruddy thing to ask but do you think you could send me a paper-back copy of "Been down so long it looks like up to me?" I had started reading it again when it walked away. If you can't, it is no sweat, but I can't get any books over here except something like Barbara Boob and Her Night with Seven Longshoremen, and stupid stuff like that. No one would read a book about dope and college riots because there is no sex in it and dope is an unmentionable evil no-no. They stick to their juice. You know, they won't let me go to Saigon to shack up. They hire private house girls for their own use since they have a lot of dust but we privates make very little dust and can't afford anything but a lay once in awhile. I hope my rapping doesn't bug you but I figure you could dig a little about what Nam is like.

I don't even know who you are and if you are a chick, I hope you can understand that I'm just unloading my mind a little.

Well, I must stop writing and start acting like I'm working to keep the lifers off my back. I hope you answer because I would really like to hear real voices of the world.

Steve

FT Dix NJ. Twelve army soldiers accused of starting a stockade riot last June have been found innocent of all charges.

Among them was Terry Klug, an avid critic of the military establishment, who was imprisoned for refusing Vietnam duty.

Seven witnesses stated that the SARE (the Army's Criminal Investigation Division) made them sign false statements under duress.

One GI, a government witness, was charged with perjury for embarrassing the prosecutor by saying, "I forgot what you told me to answer to that question."

Despite government attempts
to keep stockade conditions
out of trials, about 20
witnesses have testified about
stockade atrocities.

Black and Hispanic solidarity
in the trial helped destroy the
Army's case. About half of the
witnesses supporting Klug
were black or Puerto Rican.
Six.

"Was my dad in the War?" I asked Pete.

"Didn't he tell you the story?"

"Uh-Uh."

"It's a good one. Maybe you should let him tell it."

"Ah com'on Uncle Pete. You're here talking to me and I'm here
listening to you. You tell it."

"O.K. Your Dad was living in New Orleans.

"He was? New Orleans!"

"Yeah. He lived downtown in the French Quarters above a
nightclub. You didn't know that? But anyway, he forgot to tell his
draft board that was also in New Orleans that he'd moved back there
from Berkeley. This was just about the time we'd started to escalate
the number of people we were sending over to Nam. Lyndon
Johnson was in power and the real Vietnamese war was about to
begin. And when your dad stopped going to graduate school—he
quit for four or five months to make a few bucks, they sent him notice
of his reclassification from 1S to 1A. He didn't get the notice, of
course. Hadn't left a forwarding address in Berkeley. He also didn't

159

get the notice they mailed him nine days later telling him he was to report for his induction physical.

"So there your dad is living down in the Quarters, happy as an oyster, which he tells me he used to eat regularly while he lived there, and one morning he's closing the gate that leads into his courtyard—you know what those French Quarter buildings are like, when these two big bruisers grab him—they're U.S. Marshals. They ask him if he's Phil Good and he says, yes he is, and they ask where he's been and what he's been doing and then, this is the best part, they say "thank you" and walk away."

"They just walk away!?"

"Well, not exactly; actually, they tell him he's been reclassified and that he'd better get his affairs in order, because he'll get his shipping orders soon."

"So what does he do?"

"Well, your dad already tried once to get a commission in the Navy—when Kennedy gave that speech about 'Ask not what your country can do for you,' but the Navy turned him down because he was a Canadian."

"Then how could they draft him?"

"That was the trick. If you were a Canadian you couldn't be an officer, but you could be an enlisted man, and your dad wasn't too happy about that."

"He's not good about taking orders."

"Right. He was also not too crazy about the thought of maybe spending two years in Alaska."

"Alaska?"

"Don't ask me where your dad gets his ideas from. He didn't like the cold and he didn't like Alaska, so he figured Alaska was where the Army would send him. Anyway, he decides he'll go on down and sign up with the Coast Guard, because that way he'll at least get to spend his weekends in New Orleans. The Coast Guard's already got their quota, they say, but they put him on a waiting list. Your dad doesn't like that, but figures he can probably stall the Army until the Coast Guard gets him. Except the very next morning, when he pushes through his front gate—wham—the same two bruisers are all over him. This time, they ask him if he wouldn't mind walking with them over to the Federal Court House. Well, you know the old joke about what do you do if two eight hundred pound gorillas ask you to come down with them to the Court House. Your dad goes—they didn't put handcuffs on him or anything—but he figures he'd better not try to escape.

"Must have been a long and pleasant walk. Morning in New Orleans. Wind off the river, smell of beignets and coffee. They start off on Bourbon St, go down Conti, and then along Royal to the Court House. I can't imagine they gave your father much time to look into the windows of the antique stores. He told me he waved once, weakly, to an old friend, a lawyer, before they frog marched him inside the Federal Building, into one of the courtrooms, and sat him down on a bench.

"'Can I call a lawyer?' he says.

"'No.'

"Another U.S. Marshal enters the room and sits down behind a raised desk at the front of the room where a judge would normally sit. He's not a judge or anything—he's not wearing any robes, but he sits down there anyway. Then one of the other Marshals hollers, 'All rise, court is in session,' and boom your father is up on his feet ready for trial.

The Marshal who is serving as judge asks Phil for his name, and he says, 'Phil Good,' and then they ask him if he is the Phil Good described in the warrant and he says, 'yes, but could he have a lawyer?' The U.S. Attorney who is acting as Judge asks him if he pleads 'Not Guilty.' And Phil says again, 'could I have a lawyer, please.' The Judge says it'll be faster if you just plead 'Not Guilty,' and Phil figures what the hell, it sounds safe enough, and he's not going to get out of there unless he says it and he says, 'Not Guilty.' There's a long pause, the attorney who is up there being a judge signs a bunch of papers, and then they all get up and walk out of the court room leaving your dad just sitting there.

"'What's happening?' he cries.

"'You're free to go,' says one of the bruisers. 'But,' says your dad. 'Go,' says the bruiser.

"Your dad goes home and there's a letter and a telegram waiting for him from the Coast Guard."

"Wait a minute." I interrupt. "What is going on? Why'd they arrest Dad? Why'd they let him go?" I trusted Uncle Pete; that is, I believed the story he told me, but there was a lot about the story that did not make sense.

"I'll tell you. Let me see first if I've still got my own draft classification card. Nah, I threw it out the last time I changed wallets. I figured no one's going to draft you once you hit 50. O.K., on the back of this card where it has your draft classification, 1A or 1S or whatever, it also says in little tiny print that you've got ten days to appeal. The New Orleans Draft Board was so eager to send your dad off to Nam, they only gave him nine days. So the order for his induction was illegal. At least this is how he explained it to me. Since the order was illegal, they had to let him go. Your Dad dropped to the bottom of the lottery pile and that was the end of it. He was never drafted again."

"So he didn't have to serve?"

"Not exactly. Remember that letter and that telegram from the Coast Guard? Somehow, a friend of your dad's in New Orleans had pulled strings and got your dad off the waiting list and on to the active. The telegram told your dad he was on the active list and the letter was his orders to report for duty."

162

"In New Orleans?"

"Not exactly. What Coast Guard port is as close to the Arctic Circle as you can hope to get and still stay in the U.S.A.?"

22. Coming Home

Perhaps at this point, I should tell you how I happened to move back in with my father.

Getting in contact with him wasn't difficult. Tuesdays and Thursdays of course, he's at the University. But on every other day of the week—weekends as well as weekdays, I knew he worked in his study from dawn to almost two in the afternoon and then would go to the beach for one or two hours to surf or just to lie in the sun. "After that, I frolic," he told me, which could have meant anything, but usually involved his pursuit of one or more women, either a date or a visit to a single's bar.

He almost always went to the same stretch of beach, Lifeguard Tower 17, near 5th street, although we have half a dozen beaches near us just a short drive apart. Weekdays, he'd park adjacent to the beach and walk barefoot across the sand to his place near the tower. Weekends or whenever it was crowded, he'd park several blocks away on Pacific Coast Highway and first wear, then carry his sandals. He didn't want and wouldn't bring a beach towel. "I like to travel light," he said. So this was what I had to look for: a good-looking older man lying on the sand without a towel near Lifeguard Tower 17.

I parked on 7th Street, two blocks in from the beach. Maybe, I was unwilling to confront him directly and felt I had to kind of sneak up on our first real conversation after almost three years. Not that he'd been avoiding me, just the opposite. He'd called me frequently, inviting me to go with him to the beach, or to an art gallery, or a play at the University. That's why I knew his schedule. But I'd always said no to his invitations before.

164

I rehearsed what I was going to say to him, sort of, and the distance between 5th Street and 7th Street would give me a chance to go over it again a time or two in my mind. If he said this, then I'd say that. You know what I mean.

I'd parked close to the beach, but I carried my sandals anyway. I didn't carry a towel. I had on a bikini, my tiger with the black stripes, but I wore a man's white shirt over it with the ends tied in a knot. My hair was in a no-fuss Pixie cut.

The sea was very rough that day. Almost high tide, the spray crossed over the ridge of sand and soaked the towels of anyone unwary enough to sit close to the water. That day, most of the beach-goers were lying well back from the water's edge trying to stay warm. Warm, almost unpleasantly hot inland, the closer you got to the water, the colder you felt. Every beach-goer seeks his own personal distance from the waves and that day most of them were fifty yards in from the shore. Back close to the row of over-priced beach houses it was like a dry sauna; close to the waves where I knew my father was lying, it was like a cold day in Newfoundland or Nova Scotia.

I stayed on the ridge well away from the ocean. I've never really been comfortable in or near the water, though everyone else in my family can swim like a fish. Perhaps—I've talked about this with my shrink—it was because so much pressure was put on me when I was young to come and join the others.

A pair of male lovers lay close together on a blanket. At least, I thought they were gay until I saw the halter-top just beneath her chest on the blanket. The girl didn't have a tan line, so she must lie like that every time she came down to the beach. Her face was very close to his, their lips almost touching, and each had a hand on the other's derriere. I like that word "derriere," it's so much better than ass.

Jenny and Tara were lying side by side on their beach towels near Lifeguard Tower 16. You could tell they were lying there in the hopes

165

of being noticed by the four boys standing under the tower putting wax on their surfboards. Jenny and Tara thought they were being cool, but it was obvious what they were doing.

I noticed that Jeff Helms was one of the guys under the tower and he noticed me. "Hi Dina," he said. "Hi," I replied. Ordinarily, I'd have just kept walking, especially when I was really on my way to see my father. But I decided, just to give Jenny and Tara a hard time, to stand there for awhile and talk with Jeff and his friends. The boys weren't anything special, though Jeff looks good in a bathing suit—he's really getting muscles in his shoulders from working in his father's construction business and from surfing, of course, paddling his board out against the waves.

"Gotta go," I said after five minutes or so. "Bye Dina," the guys all said. And you could see Jenny and Tara looking over at me, hoping I would say "hi" to them and introduce them to the boys.

When I got near Lifeguard Tower 17, the situation was just the opposite. I mean now it was my father who was lying on the sand ogling all the girls. Not the girls my age—don't let me give you the impression my dad is some kind of weirdo, but not his age either. If a woman was old enough to have a kid with her, then she was old enough to arouse my father's interest and that meant some pretty young girls, 'cause how old is my father now? 45? 50?

I sat down next to him, crouched really. I wasn't going to get sand all over me the way he likes to do. Besides, who knows what kind of fleas are down there in the sand.

"Hi Di."

"Hi Dad. I'd like to come home."

And then I started to cry. O.K., so I didn't go through any of the complicated scripts I'd been rehearsing in my mind. I just wanted to come back home and live with my father. And that's what I told him.

But then, you really didn't want to know how I got back together with him, but why.

The beach is part of it. My family's life has always revolved around the beach. My dad used to say the only reason he moved here with the rents so expensive is so we could spend at least one hour each day walking on the sand. My dad would come out of his den after dinner, usually while one or the other of us kids was still washing the dishes and say, "Let's go!" meaning, "let's go now."

My mom was always quick to answer for us, "The dishes aren't done yet, are they Dina?", but Dad would reply "Oh, leave them," and then we'd all walk or bike down to the beach together.

Sometimes there would be seals, hundreds of them in the water, and sometimes a line of dolphins just beyond where the waves are breaking. The dolphins hadn't been there during the day. It was as if the dolphins and the seal men had just been waiting for the tourists to go home, too.

And, maybe, as it got darker, it would just be me and my dad walking together along the shore above the wave line, while my sisters stayed with mom and built a fire or something.

My dad talked to me then in a way he never talked with me when we were at home. He told me about his life and all he'd thought of being. He told me about the time before he met mom, when he'd been in the Coast Guard. He told me about some of the strange things he'd seen or had heard the other sailors talk about.

"There are people out there," he'd say, and he'd point beyond the line of breakers. "They look just like we do or almost, only they live under the sea. They are part man and part seal, and they herd the big fish for food, the way we herd cattle."

"Dad. You're being silly," I'd reply, scornfully. "I'm too big for stories like that." The strangest smile would come over his face. He'd look beyond me over my shoulder out to the water and say,

"Look, there's one of them, a silkie, now." And though I was too big to believe foolish stories, almost fourteen, I'd always look.

When it was very dark, and you couldn't see anything but the glow of the city and the lights of our campfire, we'd walk back and join the others. We'd have s'mores heated over the fire. We'd talk about what we'd done during the day. And then we'd go back home together.

Of course, as I got older, I spent less time with my family or, at least, I tried to. I had a life of my own, I thought. At school and with my friends. Then came the time, my crazy period, I call it now, when I had nothing at all to do with my family, when I hated them. When I hung out at the beach with Jeff and Don and the others. When all I did was hang out and I didn't go to school.

I began by ditching class. And when the school called my parents in and said she's been ditching, I said, "Well, if I have to go to Spanish—(I think that was the class I'd been cutting)—well, I won't go to school at all."

And I didn't. I spent all day at the pier hanging out and sometimes I'd be at there in the evening, too.

Mom and Dad tried to make a place for me. Mom tried harder. Dad insisted I do things the way Dana and Donna had done, especially Dana. "You have to study," he said, "It's a new competitive world out there. If you were Chinese or Japanese, I'd be making you study, tying you to that chair until all your homework was done."

"Oh, let her have some fun," Mom would say, "She's only young once."

"That's just the point," Dad would persist, "there's just too much competition, today. The kids no longer have the time to be young."

My mom and dad would argue then and they would be arguing long after my sisters and I had shut our bedroom doors and pretended to be asleep.

Eventually my mother came to me and said, "I'm moving out. Do you want to come with me?'

"Sure," I said, "Will I get my own room?"

So I moved in with my mom, but that really didn't work out. Donna moved in, too, and I had the same problems sharing a room with her that I'd had before.

I started cutting class again. Mom talked to the principal and they decided to send me to one of the alternative schools. It was easier than the regular school; I just had to go there in the mornings. My dad came to the school to protest but there was nothing he could do about it.

I went to the alternative school sometimes and sometimes I didn't. I got arrested—don't ask me what for, and I smoked a lot of dope, which was crazy because I've always been against drugs. I started staying over nights at different people's places and then I just didn't bother to come home. It was my mom's place anyway, not mine.

Sometimes, I went to the beach by myself, not often. Usually, I went with another girl, or with the group. If I went by myself, I would park my bike under a street lamp and then head into the darkness between the houses toward the beach.

You're almost blind when you leave the streetlights. The sea is still a phosphorescent glimmer off in the distance and it takes a while before you can even make out shadows. I always walk slowly and carefully. I don't want to stumble or fall in the sand. I don't want somebody jumping at me out of the darkness, not even a friend. I stop every few feet and listen.

Sometimes all you can hear is the wind. Other times, you might hear a voice, perhaps two voices, though you can't tell where the voices are coming from. It could be a couple sitting nearby in the darkness or a pair of joggers striding side by side further away along the shore.

A jogger runs by me on the bike path and I move out of his way, startled. The wind changes direction. All at once, I can smell the sea and hear the waves. I stand for a long while in the stillness, just breathing the air, becoming one with the sea and the sand.

A loud splash comes from directly in front of me. I can hear the sound of something large moving in the water, but I can't see what it is. For an instant, a cigarette glows in the darkness, or maybe it is a campfire rekindled by the wind. I strain my eyes and look out toward the water. I still cannot see anything when a door opens behind me in one of the beach houses and a shaft of light reaches out over the waves.

For a moment all is still, and then—splash—a big fish—it's a dolphin, leaps almost straight up against the light.

Splash and the dolphin is gone, and then I walk back to my bicycle and peddle home.

There are shops down by the pier—army surplus, not-quite-in-style clothing, restaurants where you can get three grade-C eggs and a stack of pancakes for $1.98. I must have worked in all of them. They're used to employees that come and go.

I worked during the day, of course. The day belongs to the kids and maybe the tourists. A wave of surfers hits the beaches for an hour or two before school starts. By nine, they've disappeared and it's time for the bums to have breakfast. Nine or ten and the buses from inland begin to unload office workers and laborers who've taken the day off to get a tan. Two o'clock, school's out, and the second wave of surfers appears.

I used to go down to the pier regularly between two and five, we all did. There would always be someone there to talk to. I'd stay on till seven or eight sometimes, but usually I would leave before it got dark.

It is different by the pier after it is dark. The sky goes from bright blue to gray, the streetlights come on, and then, all of a sudden, there is a vacancy, a big dark hole where the sea has been. The crazies show up then and the heavies, too, fresh from tapping the source. They look you up and down as if you were a piece of meat and they hit on you or, if you are skinny like me, they ask you for money or get you to do errands.

What they mean by errands is making a dope delivery. The money would already have changed hands or maybe the dope and you'd be carrying a package they know you are too afraid to open. I was afraid, too, that one day a policeman would stop me and I would go to jail. Or, like so many of my friends, that the police would turn me into a snitch and then I would always be afraid of everyone.

The pier is a frightening place after dark. The night I'm telling you about, a week before I went back to live with my father, this Spanish guy, elegant in a white linen suit, parks his big white Cadillac next to where I'm standing. He gets out of the Cadillac, not speaking, leans against his car and looks out the length of the pier toward an invisible ocean. I wonder what he is thinking. There are street lamps on the pier, maybe every two or three hundred feet, but there are long dark stretches in between and no one goes out on the pier after dark.

Then this Spanish dude is standing next to me. "Kid," he says, "you take this ten bucks; you watch my car." I nod my head; I don't say anything. And he walks out on the pier.

He never comes back. After awhile, when two of my friends drive by wanting to know what is happening, I let them drive me home.

23. Psychodrama IV

"Did they ever get to you in a psychodrama, Dad? I mean, you ran away that one time."

"Ran away? Are you talking about that amateur night in Menlo Park you read about in my diary? I didn't run away, I walked away. The whole amateur-night thing didn't make any sense.

"Yes, I went back; more than once; actually; it was a cheap Friday night date in those days to go to Chung's psychodramas. There would be upwards of a hundred people at them sometimes; you could participate or you could just watch as most of us did, though often, without you realizing it, you'd find yourself drawn into the action.

"But they never got to me there. Too many other people to choose from. I learned a lot though, watching, enough to run my own psychodramas. Mostly, what I learned was to be conscious of and to experience my own feelings."

I gave him the look.

"O.K., I'm not perfect even now, but I did learn enough to run my own gigs.

"I remember one night at Chung's, this Merchant Marine walked in. He was bare foot; he wore a tight fitting pair of pants and a short sleeve shirt that fit him, just, across his broad chest with the top two buttons unbuttoned. He stood on the mat, hands crossed at his waist, his bare feet planted beneath him like a tall oak tree. That was the expression Chung used when he saw him standing there, 'like a tall oak.' I was never that centered. But this guy was a natural, not someone who'd learned about life though books or by playing at psychodrama but by living it.

"Chung stopped the psychodrama when he saw him and we all just looked at the guy. He smiled and we smiled back.

"I'll be honest with you, I always wanted to be at the center working, having Chung pay attention to me. I'd just pretend to be watching a lot of the time, but inside I was seething, working on my own imaginary script.

"I think if Chung had called on me, I would have done well, changed faster than I did later. I'd learned to Chung by that time: to bellow with rage, to cry—almost on command, to know my feelings, if not to feel them.

"'You know what you feel, but you don't feel it.' was what he said to me that day."

"Who? Chung? Chung told you that?"

My dad paused. You could see the memories going through his head. "No. Robb. Robb Crist, but that was later, at the marathon."

Dad stopped talking, hung his head, and, for a moment, retreated inside himself. I was conscious then that there was almost as much gray as black in my dad's hair and that his jowls were heavier than they had been, were beginning to droop like those of moo grandma.

"Tell me about it, Dad."

"I don't want to. I don't like to admit to those parts of me that are really bad."

"Bad?"

"All right, not bad—evil, bad—inadequate. The fear. I'm afraid of some things. I'm afraid of dying, Dina. Or, I was afraid then. I'm not sure I am now. Now, I'm afraid I'll lose my job; I won't be able to afford medical insurance. I'll lose this house; I won't have any place to stay.

"When you kids were still in the crib, your mom and I would wake up in the middle of the night to check your breathing. I'd touch your cheek: warm, listen carefully for the sigh, the quick inrush of breath, you'd exhale finally, sleepily—you were alive.

"When you started going to school, I'd still make the rounds at night, checking that the windows and the doors were locked, checking that you were safe in your bed. Mainly, it was in the daytime that we'd worry. Had there been an accident? Had the school bus skidded on the rain-slick road and gone over into a ravine? Remember, I taught you what to do if the school bus bogged down in a snowdrift and it was the exact opposite of what the school had told you to do."

"You and mom were always overprotective." I broke in.

"Your mother and I were always scared. But you're alive today aren't you and you're pretty together?"

"Yeah, Dad. But I don't want to talk about myself now."

A long pause followed. We'd stopped talking, again. I could tell he was thinking, all right Dina, you've been home for a month now, when are you going to talk? Not yet Dad, please. You talk.

"Tell me about your psychodrama Dad, about the time they got to you."

Throughout the first long night, several people took turns at "working" through their problems. Mainly women at first. Then the men. One woman had broken up with her husband and wanted to go back to him, but was afraid things would all go wrong again. One girl wanted her father to tell her he loved her, and an older woman, she might have been in her late forties, came forward and said—this was unexpected—she wanted her father to love her, too. The two women hugged each other.

One after the other, like walking letters to Aimai Cristen, the people around me played through the various parts as they had at the Amateur Night Psychodrama.

"My wife walked out on me," George said; the tone of his voice suggested loneliness, despair.

"He's a real nowhere man," sang the Beetles in the background.

Someone, a girl, asked George why he fooled around.

"I like women, that's not unusual," he proclaimed. His despairing tone had vanished to be replaced by a certain smug triumph.

"But do you like men?"

"What kind of a question is that?" And George's smugness had given way to anger.

"Answer it then," a girl with a truly unpleasant braying voice commanded.

"I'm getting out of here." It was more a question than a statement.

"You're not going anywhere." And they all piled on him, pining his thighs and shoulders to the carpeted floor.

Would George change? Probably. Did I care? Ah, that was the question. I'd heard too much, seen too much by then.

A lot of what we heard that first night was repetitious. People talked around their problems, offered excuses, admitted guilt, perhaps, in the end, but for the wrong crimes.

We'd heard it all before, many times, at Chung's, and thus the shock value was gone, though the inevitable progression of denial, anger, and, finally, hope seemed to strike each of those confessing as novel and terrifying. Most of us harbor a secret and false belief that if we only let ourselves go, cast off the civilized restraints and gave way to our anger, we would destroy everything and everyone around us. But we can't, you know. We really are as helpless as children in so many ways. We can only act and talk so as to cut down the odds against us.

Those of us on the outskirts of the melodrama talked and flirted and sometimes danced to the rock music in the background. The Airplane's "We Should Be Together" from their Volunteers of America album was one of the most popular dance tunes then. When we danced, we danced in groups. We didn't touch, except accidentally, but we tried to shape our pattern to the other person's.

(And why was someone as solitary as I so interested in togetherness? I should have known then that I was hiding. Hoping that for the three long days and the two long nights of the marathon I would stay concealed in the background.)

"You in the background, Dad? You, who is almost totally unwilling to be a spectator."

"I was trying to stay in the background, all right? Checking my impulses. Anticipating and reacting so quickly that no one could spot my hesitation. Ask me what I felt, I might say, 'anger,' and as that feeling was displaced, 'sorrow,' or 'fear,' or 'hate, ' letting my psyche serve as its own inspector. 'That's Six,' they'd say, 'doing his thing.' Some people liked me as Six. Some didn't. No one knew who Phil Good was."

I was able to stay in hiding through most of the second day. True, I fought on a couple of occasions—wrestling matches, more of a workout than anything really in anger. I had been challenged, usually by a much younger man. And though I knew that fighting was childish, wrong, I felt I had to fight. Chung's rules, of course. No hitting, except with an open palm. Stop immediately on command from the facilitator.

The fight would always begin as a simple test of strength and then the anger would come boiling up from inside, violent, uncontrollable.

There was one exception: a fight that wasn't, a fight, where I chose—consciously—to embrace my opponent rather than to attack him.

The center of attention was this German graduate student, or perhaps he was some sort of professor. (You don't like Germans, do you Dad?) I didn't know his name. I must have been away when he joined the Free U. He'd pushed himself to the front quickly and now fancied himself a second Chung. I didn't like him particularly, but he had mastered the Chungian dialectic, could convey genuine feeling. He was good at doubling, getting inside people's heads, expressing what they were feeling or what the crowd thought they should feel. Some people liked him. I thought he was a hypocrite.

Of course, some people like me too, just as I know there are some who don't.

Somehow, this German had taken over one of the encounters—we had sort of three-ring circus going on the second morning, with several individuals "working" in different parts of the room and the fellow at the record player going crazy trying to provide a suitable background for all three at once.

The German's notion of an psychodrama was a wrestling match in which he would hold the other fellow or woman down, slap them across the face a couple of times and get

177

them to admit their real problem was not some other person but themselves.

I don't know how I got lured into a direct confrontation with him but I did. I refused to wrestle, however, or to take turns, kneeling on the floor, bashing and being bashed at with an open hand; instead, after taking my licks, I leaned forward— the pacifist's approach and brushed his lips with mine. He shoved me away angrily and began to wrestle. I only hugged him tighter, deliberately thinking and feeling all the while, I love you, I love you, how I wish you loved me too.

"You cock sucker," he shouted when his wrestling proved fruitless and he was unable to put me on the floor. True, I was on my knees and he stood erect, but I wasn't down.

I grasped his knees. He shoved me away and repeated the coarse epithet.

I stuck my tongue out at him.

"You fag," he bellowed. But he didn't get to me with this. Not in that company. My sexuality was one area in which I felt secure.

"I could use a hug," I said as I had that one time at the meeting of Boy Scout mothers. But he merely cursed me roundly and walked away.

My round, believe it or not, by the standards we employed then. I'd remained centered, though my hair and clothing were all mussed. He'd been thrown off balance and had to walk away. But I'd lost too, by allowing my acting to substitute for genuine feeling.

I'd shown the nonviolent approach was feasible, that you didn't have to be violent to win, but I hadn't persuaded him or anyone else to like me because of it. And, perhaps, deep inside, I hadn't yet persuaded myself to like him. My decision

178

to embrace, rather than to fight him had come from my reason, not my heart.

A lot of crying, a lot of screaming. Quiet times, too, and breaks for meals. Oh, and a lot of comic relief.

One slightly overweight girl—Amy? Annie?—had been sitting next to me on and off throughout the first day of the marathon. She was cute, or would be if she lost a little weight, and I was always trying to get her to talk to me. She'd say, 'Shh, I'm trying to listen,' and when I persisted she'd just move away.

The second day of the marathon she complained about me to the group: 'Every time I sit down next to Phil he makes a pass at me.'

'Then why do you sit down next to him?' the entire room hollered as one.

The rest of the humor was subtler. Like this one girl, a nurse, 'the nurse' we called her eventually, who started out fully clothed, almost overdressed, given the warm weather and the casual clothing the rest of us were wearing, and gradually started taking off her clothes item by item.

When we took turns massaging each other, she was the first to take off all her clothes. And she didn't put them back on, not for the entire three days of the marathon. She had an absolutely fantastic body. I guess she'd just been waiting for an excuse to take her clothes off, for 'permission' as Mary-Ellen, my Catholic friend would say. She'd been keeping that gorgeous body covered up for years in some kind of uniform and now, at last she was ready to say, 'here I am.'

Big breasts. No, enormous ones. D's at least and firm. I don't recall her working through anything—not with words the way the rest of us were condemned to do. But I'm sure that what the nurse wanted, needed to do, she did: she took her clothes off and showed everyone how great she looked and how good she felt about herself.

It was an honest feeling. That was the most important thing in those days, to get in touch with and express your real feelings.

Dad paused. I could tell he was back inside his head again, remembering. "You know, at the end, Robb said to me, 'You know exactly how you feel or how you're supposed to feel, but you don't ever really feel it.'

'You don't ever let your feelings get to you.'"

Dad shook his head. Were there tears in his eyes?

I said, "We talked about that once in the twelve-step program. People who know their feelings but can't, won't experience them."

I paused. Dad had stopped talking and was watching me intently, listening, really listening to what I had to say, and I couldn't say another word. After awhile, he put his arm around my shoulders and resumed speaking. Was he holding me or was I holding him?

About an hour or so before the end of the marathon, the facilitator—yes there was one, although he'd remained in the background for most of the weekend—suggested we go around the room and one by one summarize what we felt we had got out of the experience.

When it came my turn to speak, someone put on a record, the Kinks singing 'A Well Respected Man:

He gets up in the morning,

and he goes to work at nine.'

I leveled with them and told them that I'd been trying to stay in the background and avoid my usual tendency to make myself the center of attention.

"Like your fight with Carl," someone said. "And the passes you've been making at Amy," added another. "I had two fights with him," said a tall lean college student, sandy-haired and Scots by the look of him. (We'd had two fights, wrestling matches, and I'd won them both.)

"You don't seem to have been trying very hard 6," Robb said, "Fighting with Carl. Amy's not the only girl who's complained to me about your hands. Whenever I looked around, you seemed to be in the middle of things, stirring them up."

'He's oh so good.

He's oh so fine.

He's oh so healthy

In his body and his mind,' sang the Kinks.

I could take criticism from the others easily, but Robb was my friend. "You're making fun of me," I said.

"Why not, you're a ridiculous jerk."

I looked stricken—deliberately, playing for laughs to the crowd, but actually, I was angry. Robb was my friend. Had been ever since I joined the Free-U. In place of the expected sympathy—we'd been together for three days after all, I was getting sarcasm from him, indifference from the others.

The room fell silent. At a time when I most wanted to be left alone, the marathon almost over, an hour or so for quiet and reflection and then escape, I'd suddenly become the center of attention. I'm sure that mine was only one of several groups and yet in an instant, I felt alone, facing a room full of accusers.

"We could fight again," said Sandy, the young Scot I'd wrestled with before. He stood up and I stood up. He pushed me and I pushed back and then, all of a sudden, I didn't feel like fighting anymore. I withdrew into my shell, curled up, literally, physically, inside myself. I am nothing: you could see it in my face.

"Asshole." "Wimp."   A girl's hand whipped out, and flicked my testicles.

"Stop that," I hollered.

Sandy, still confronting me, reached out a hand and shoved me in the chest. Behind him, I could see Robb egging him on.

"Stop that, you don't know what you're doing!" I hollered. He pushed me again and I pushed back.

Push. Push. Sandy deliberately turned his back on me and started to walk away. "What a wimp," he said to no one in particular.

The man he'd been confronting, my God it was I, gave a blood-curdling scream and leaped on Sandy's back, flailing away. Immediately, I was seized from behind and wrestled to the floor. Four men sat on my arms and my legs. I recognized their faces. "Bastards," I cried. Sandy sat astride my chest, began to slap my face rhythmically. Someone put an arm over my mouth. I tried to bite them.

"MMph." The arm came from an unseen figure in back of me and to the side. It coiled around my neck, cradling my

182

head, cutting off the air supply. The hand expanded until it covered my nose as well as my mouth. "MMph," I tried to say.

I couldn't breathe. Because of the hand. I twisted but could not dislodge it. "You wanted to die, Phil," Robb said, "then die."

Robb's voice. No, not Robb. Robb is my friend; Robb wouldn't hurt me. I want Robb to hug me, want Robb to take care of me. I tried to cry, but couldn't get the air, I was choking. . . .

All my life I have been afraid of dying. When I was five, just before I started school, I would keep myself awake at night, pinching myself, rubbing saliva into my eyes, not wanting to sleep, afraid that while I was asleep, I would die, and then there would be no more me.

I could die now, easily. All I had to do was let go and relax. It would be like it had been that week with the flu when I was eighteen, alive, but barely, floating in and out of consciousness.

When I was dead, and no longer a threat, my father would let me live.

Colors rose before my eyes, pinwheels of light, the same long tunnel that had been there the night of the concert at the Family Dog. And amidst the colors, Sandy's face.

"I want to live!" I cried, sitting up despite the pressure on my chest and arms. It was a new voice, a different, deeper, more powerful voice. I put all my force, all my strength, into a single arm and a single blow at the face before me. Sandy tumbled backwards, surprised.

"I want to live!" I said.

Robb's face was only inches from my own. "Do it. Stop thinking about dying and put your energy into being alive." Robb paused, "Do you know what you feel?"

"I feel angry. I feel powerful. I feel . . ."

"You know how you feel, but do you let yourself feel it?" Robb asked, and each of the faces around me echoed the question. They were no longer the faces of a mob; each and every one belonged to a separate individual. I started to live. I started to feel.

Brother Beware

Somebody at the Message Information Center, San Diego's switchboard, is fucking with people's minds and pocket books.

A San Diego mother phoned MIC to report that one of her fourteen-year old twin daughters was missing again and to ask if MIC would act as a contact.

Sure, she was told, "But it would cost money." (Note: MIC services are free, though donations are welcomed.)

The contact from MIC called back shortly to report. In all, he was to call her sixteen or seventeen times about her daughter, sometimes at three or four in the morning. He had a lead, he said, but it would cost money to follow it up.

How much money?

"Two hundred dollars."

Sometimes, the woman confided to BARB, the amount was only one hundred or fifty dollars. Once she said, it was two thousand! Always there was a hot lead. Incredibly, no money ever changed hands.

"I was scared. My husband is away in Viet Nam. It's such a funny sound when the phone is ringing in the early morning and you're all alone in the house."

Bonnie, that's the runaway, returned the other day. She had never heard from the friendly switchboard man, although she had used MIC frequently to stay in contact with her friends.

There have been other complaints. Let's find this guy and trash him. #6

Right Now's How

There's no more clean air left in the United States. That's the word coming down over the AP wires this Sunday. And so, with apologies to Phil Ochs:

I go to pollution rallies

and I put down the
combustion car

I hate plastic disposable beer
cans

Hope industrial wastes won't
spread from the tar

But don't ask me to sacrifice
comfort

That's going a little bit too far

Love me, love me, love me

I'm an ecowimp — #6

The Neighborhood Committees

Are you over thirty? Look
straight? Own your own
home? Has the Neighbor-
hood Committee been to see
you yet?

A listener to WEBN in
Cincinnati (underground rock
for seven hours, seven nights
a week) called the station to
say he'd been approached at
his home in Lexington KY by
just such a group. These
good old boys held weekend
training drills with live ammo

as a possible precaution against possible invasion by hippies and other terrorists.

The Neighborhood Committee does more than recruit. In Hamburg NY, the Committee invited the occupants of a commune to leave or get burned out. A head shop that the owner says was more antiques than psychedelic paraphernalia also closed in response to threats.

There is no Committee yet in Woodstock NY but the neighboring villages are so organized. There's no Committee in your neighborhood is there? Sir? #6

Clearance Creekwater Revival

I joined the ecology action group today in a clearance creekwater revival. The plan was to do something about the pollution found in many of our country's streams and rivers.

The evidence of destruction
is in every streambed: broken
glass, pottery shards, barbed
wire, insulators, and various
found objects.

But the cure proved to be
worse than the disease: The
crowd went at Cordonices
Creek in North Berkeley like
the Army Corps of Engineers
dredging a canal. They ripped
up the streambed, dislodged
stepping stones and plants;
they dug and they filled; they
lined the creek with concrete
chunks so the banks wouldn't
erode. They built dams!

"Leave the stream bed
alone," a young man identified
only as Lorne cried; but we
couldn't hear him; we were
too busy getting our pictures
taken, or taking pictures, or
getting interviewed by KQED.

I started off picking bits of
glass from the sand and, later,
advanced to raker that gave
me the opportunity to stir up
the loam and gravel for
someone else to sift through.
We started upstream and
worked our way down with the

result that it became more and more difficult to see the effects of what we were doing through the muddy water.

A press gang put me aboard a truck that was traveling between the different revival sites consolidating refuse. I noted during these travels that there was yet more refuse scattered on the lawns of the homes near our work sites— lunch bags, cigarette butts, newspapers, and rally announcements. At our destination, a crew worked at separating junk from compost. Not so much to get at the compost, which was destined for People's Park, as to form a pile of beer cans and found objects for the TV cameras.

After lunch at MacDonald's (free refreshments were to have been provided by the ecology action coordinators, yes they were, oh yes) I joined with a splinter group and went about crying "volunteers" until I succeeded in volunteering five carloads of workers, three cars, a VW microbus, rakes, shovels and many other instruments of destruction. Then, my group drove to the Berkeley Rose Garden.

Cordonices Creek flows through Indian Rock Park, ducks under the Rose Garden, follows an aqueduct through three elegant back yards, bobs underground again and reappears as a waterfall right in the center of the largest, weed-ridden, unkempt estate in all of Berkeley. In the course of tracing the stream's elusive progress, we gathered our usual quota of old newspapers, discarded cigarette packs, and beer cans. I asked a middle-aged man raking his lawn if he had a garbage can in which we could toss the accumulation. "No," is all he said.

Beneath the waterfall, the stream was clear and sparkling. A few pieces of glass could be removed from the bottom and some scrap iron. Great hunks of iron that weighed forty to seventy-five pounds each—part of a wheel and what looked to be a muffler if they made mufflers without a bore. Lugging those pieces up the side of the ravine to the road was not fun.

(Oops. I just remembered I was suppose to tell someone to tell the truck to come pick up all the garbage we left stacked on Spruce street. Sorry. Hope some kind person hauled the garbage away.)

Cordonices Creek also runs through Live Oak Park. Finding a game of revolutionary volleyball was in progress when we got to the Park, I dropped out of the Creekwater Revival to join the game.

But I guess I can drop in again any time. I don't really need an ecology-action coordinator to tell me what to do. I survived the day without buses, free refreshments, or rock bands. All I need to do it again is a pair of gloves, a rake, maybe, and a box or a burlap bag. And a polluted stream: but they're not hard to find — #6.

24. Altamont

As I got nearer to the bottom of the boxes, it became more and more evident to me that my mom and dad came from two different countries. She was a college dropout who thought herself a failure not because she was a failure at school—she was too conscientious to let that happen—but because she hadn't been accepted in the sorority her mother and her aunts had belonged to. He was a double Ph.D. My mom looks like Doris Day; my dad's hair is always windblown and when he puts on his white lab coat, you just know that he and his assistant Igor are going to assemble a monster that afternoon.

"It sounds like you two had absolutely nothing in common," I said to my dad one day, "I mean, you and mom tell completely different stories about the sixties. She talks about her sorority and the time she worked in the Nixon campaign. You..."

But he'd already interrupted, "Nixon? Can you believe it! I'm a Yippie—at least after Bobby died—and she works for Nixon. That's why we broke up finally."

"After eighteen years."

"Eighteen years. It was you kids that held us together."

"We didn't do too good a job."

"You did great. I enjoyed those years. I'm having a good time now. Thanks for being here."

My dad's hair is almost all gray now. He looks almost angelic with his big euphoric smile. I could tell by the smile that he was still thinking about those years when we were a family. No, I was wrong.

He was thinking about something that had happened before that, when he first met mom.

"I met her down here in Pasadena when I moved back to L.A. again. Got a job at the Jet Propulsion Laboratory. Did I tell you your mom made the best coffee on my floor, the best in the building, and she wore that cute little stewardess outfit, I mean that apron, whenever she made coffee?"

I nodded as if I knew what my dad was talking about. As he spoke, you could tell he was reliving the best part of his time with mom, or the next to best. But then, all of a sudden, the smile left his face, and he looked old and worn. Was he thinking about the divorce, the year afterwards when I was gone, or the year of fighting just before the breakup? It took me several minutes after he'd began to speak again to realize he was not criticizing, not delegating blame, but thinking about something else entirely, something that had happened long before I was born.

"There were two reasons why I left the Bay Area and the whole underground scene. Two reasons. They killed that cop. And Altamont."

"Tell me about Altamont," I begged. I didn't want to hear about the killing, though I knew he would tell me both stories and in his own way.

"You've already read about Altamont," he began. I shook my head. "Well then, you've seen the movie *Gimmie Shelter*?" I shook my head a second time. "Well, I still won't give you all the gory details. You can pick them up by renting the video. Suffice it to say that for a week before the concert, the radio had been trumpeting about how the Rolling Stones were coming to the Bay Area to do a free concert. It would be another Woodstock, another summer of love."

194

The concert was scheduled originally for Golden Gate Park, the place where they'd had the first Human Be-In, back when it all began. But then they couldn't get a concert permit from the City of San Francisco, so they moved the concert somewhere else. They moved the location three or four times and you just had to keep listening to the FM to figure out where it was going to be held. By the time the Barb went to press for the week, we still didn't know where the free concert would be. Eventually, the organizers relocated it to some racetrack in the valley, along route 5, redneck county, which may explain the kind of people that showed up at the concert and the way they behaved.

I was staying overnight in Pete's apartment with a friend. He hadn't invited me to stay exactly, but I still had a copy of his key and I knew he was out of town. Just like Pete, the biggest concert of the decade and he was somewhere else.

Getting there was fun. (Getting back wasn't.) City dude goes to country, singing from Beetle's songbook, while girlfriend drives. Part one led us through the usual lace of Interstates, over the Berkeley Hills, then into Terra Incognito. The second part was a state road; four lanes turned into two; the traffic slowed, became stop and go. Two miles from the concert site, we could already see where cars were parking, though we couldn't see anything that resembled the Altamont Raceway. I saw a couple of cars take a dirt trail through a meadow that disappeared over a hill. "Let's try it," I said to Fanny or Sally or whatever her name was. (A really nice girl by the way, I'm just blanking on her name.)

The trail through the hills brought us forward another mile, but then we had no choice but to park as the trail became a dozen paths each terminating in a single parking space. (Later, of course, people were even parking between the spaces, but we had arrived near the beginning of the concert.)

195

I wondered at the time what the farmers who owned the land thought about all the cars that were parking on their property. The next week's newspapers brought the answer: he, they, were suing the owners of the Altamont Speedway for damages.

A wonderful sunny day told me I was lucky to be alive. The trail from the parking lot soon joined with other trails, so that we were walking three or four abreast when we came to the top of the rise. Just like in the Joni Mitchell song "Woodstock" that Crosby, Stills and Nash made popular, about the stream of people who walked through the hills to form the Woodstock Nation. But if Woodstock hailed the new enlightenment, the resurrection and the life, then Altamont was the black mass.

A cloud of smoke hung over the valley. Not cigarettes. A different brand. It took three shampoos the next day to finally get the smell out of our hair.

Guys were clinging to the wooden towers the concert promoters had erected to hold the lights and sound equipment. Throughout the concert, you could hear the promoters screaming over the public address system, "Come down from the towers. It is too dangerous. Come down from there." But however many they chased away, there were always more to take their place, and nothing could dislodge the guys who had already climbed to the top of the towers and sat there throughout the afternoon drinking beer and, later, urinating into the crowd.

You all know who played at the concert—a couple of warm up bands I'm not sure of—the Flying Burrito Brothers?—I may be wrong on that one—now, you're going to check out the cassette and say, "Dad's a liar; he wasn't there at all"—The Airplane—they were terrible. That's because there was all this fighting. Between the Hell's Angels and the people who were standing just in front of the stage. The Angels had been hired to keep people off the stage and away from the bands. I danced on stage at an Airplane concert once, at the Winterland, and Bill Graham himself threw me off the platform.

The Hell's Angels got a little rambunctious—they were a poor choice for security to begin with, and one of them even whacked Marty Balin, the Airplane's lead singer, in the head. Now, we were all crazy about Grace Slick in those days, and if she'd have said, "Kill the Angels," we probably would of; because however tough the Hells Angels were and however many weapons they had, there were hundreds of thousands of us. Those numbers were part of the problem. The valley the concert was held in tapered inward as you moved toward the stage. So that if the ten thousand people in the last row at the back of the natural amphitheater each moved forward an inch, the hundred or so people in the front row were virtually thrown forward thirty feet across the stage. Whereupon the Hell's Angels would start bashing their heads and shoulders with pool cues.

But Grace didn't say kill, she said, "Love. Press against them with your bodies. Show them love." So we did. At least the people in the front rows who were near the Angels tried to, but the Angels just kept flailing away at them with their pool cues and whacked anyone who was foolish enough to come close.

Back in the center of the valley, about row 300 where Sally and I and Robb Crist and a few others from the Free U were located, a single dot on some pointillist's conception, we lay on the grass, propped up against one another, eating grapes and other munchies. It wasn't one of those concerts where you could walk around and go from one group of friends to another. Too many people were crammed into the same limited space. But we stayed mellow, not because we were smoking grass—a lot of marijuana was being passed from hand to hand, and group to group—but because there was so much marijuana smoke already in the air. This was preNixon, when grass was cheap, a toke was something you shared, and a friend was any person who sat next to you; in the decade to come, Nixon would turn the marijuana trade over to the Mafia in return for their financial support in his election.

The Stones took too long to get onstage at the concert. They wanted to make a grand entrance. The result was just too much dead time between the last warm-up band and the Stones' first appearance on stage. The delay meant more fighting and more drinking beer in the hot sun, neither of which went with a new "Summer of Love." But then, as I already told you, Altamont was the Concert of Hate.

Maybe, that's not really a surprise. These were the Stones after all. Where the Beetles poo-pooed the anger in, "You talk about revolution, well, I'd like to see the plan," the Stones had their Street Fighting Man. And the Stone's entrance into Street Fighting Man that day was probably the tightest, most meaningful version of the song they ever performed. But the intensity didn't last; the Stones hadn't gone more than sixteen bars, when Jagger was on the microphone begging, "People, People, what's going on? Why are you fighting with each other? Why are you fighting?" And then of course—the killing took place just about this time—the Stones had to pull back; Mick signaled to Keith to Muzak the rhythms, drag the beat enough so you wouldn't feel the pounding in your veins. For some of us, the pounding was the end in itself, but for the beer-drinking rowdies, the pounding rhythm of the Stones was the longed-for pretext to pound and beat up on their fellow man.

It was a bad concert. After the Stones, there was nothing, no entertainer to keep you in your seat a little longer, an after-concert concert like they have today at some of the football games to slow the exit from the stands. Just the murmur of the departing crowd, and an impression of dampness as the fog began to settle down on the valley. They say almost three-quarters of a million people were in that walk out of the valley and in the lines of cars that stretched across the hills and merged and merged again until we were one solid mass upon the highway.

I heard later that people driving from LA to San Fran along Interstate 5 that evening didn't know what hit them. Without any warning, they were part of a massive traffic jam and spent up to four hours on that short section of road, sometimes without moving, just barely inching forward. If they were clever, they left the freeway, had dinner, and maybe an extra dessert. I let Lynn drive, I think Lynn was her name. We talked. We listened to the radio. An entire hour was devoted to Dylan. "And while the King was looking down." We had a very pleasant time. But I don't think Lynn and I saw each other more than three or four times after that.

25. Letters to Aimai Cristen, Part III

Dear Aimai: [written on hotel stationary]

I've never been a sugar daddy before.

I'm an industrial sales manager. A sponsor to a young 24-year old, I'd love to be part of. If...

If you're sincere and not a 'hustler,' I'll give you two-thirds of what I have. But put me on—and I'll spit in your eye.

If you check me out, I'll be glad to tell you about my college career and its financial struggle. Then the G.I. bill entered the scene. Free education by Uncle Sam. Girl, it's the best!!!

Aimai, you could be a big fat fake. It's happened before! But if you are sincere and IF you want companionship, conversation, good films and financial help call me at my very square office — 555-8383. Just ask for me and play it by ear.

I've just moved back from Hollywood and I have no home phone because I expect to relocate. But if you knock on my door any nite after 7:00 P.M, I assure you no wife will answer.

I'm in no hurry Aimai. Answer all those eager beavers first.

Bob

\#

Barb Beats Oinkers

San Francisco Municipal Judge Albert Axelrod took the SF PD to task Wednesday for the improper arrest of a BARB vendor who spent a totally unnecessary night in jail.

Vendor John Catron was picked up at 4:50 Wednesday afternoon in front of the

Greyhound Depot for "vending within 12 feet of a public building."

"The statue in question," the Judge said, "applies only to the selling of tickets for entertainment."

The Judge then dismissed all charges, advising John to inform the police officers of this ruling before they made any further "errors."

The error in question cost John a night in city jail, plus 11 BARBS and a pocketknife ripped off by the pigs.

BARB does not intend to allow any of its vendors to be hassled. If hassled, call BARB immediately at 849-1040, -1041, or -1046.   #6

26. The Killing

"You've got to understand my relationship with the Barb.

"I didn't work there full time. In fact, we were all part timers. A graduate student in journalism worked with us once—we were his thesis project; he said we were the only newspaper in the country staffed entirely by part timers, and the only newspaper where the staff did rewrites. We weren't really journalists, you see, at least we weren't when we started. So, we kind of thought on paper, instead of organizing the material in our minds first, the way real newspaper people do who have to work against a deadline.

"The Barb was a weekly, which made us kind of a cross between a magazine and a daily newspaper. Most of our stories were written well in advance, so there was time for rewrites. Some stories could only be written at the last moment, like if you got a letter from the Weatherman Underground on the evening of the deadline, but I never worked on those. I had some of my best stories killed because they were bumped by something more topical. Like the time I discovered who trashed the printing press belonging to this underground newspaper in San Diego. It was the cops, themselves, would you believe it? The State finally got around to prosecuting the policemen once Nixon was out of office and all their protection vanished. But my story and an early trial got set aside when Dr. Tim (Leary) turned up just before press time at the Barb with a new 'world revelation.'

"Anyhow, the weekend of the killing, I'd been finishing up in the laboratory and wasn't able to leave Bodega much before nine. In the end, I stayed overnight and headed out for Berkeley the next morning. I really wasn't in Berkeley when it happened. And then I had to read about the killing in the Gazette first, because we weren't due out till the next day.

"I found out later—it's one of those ironies of life, only a not very amusing one—that the two killers had planned the murder so the story would appear first in the Barb along with their letter of explanation. Only the killers got it wrong; Tuesday was the day we went to press, not Wednesday, which was when we distributed the papers, unless you count the occasional week in which we'd hand the paper out to our carriers at a quarter to midnight the day before.

"That was always one weird scene—when we gave the papers to the carriers. A lot of people that did smack sold the Barb. It was a lot less risky way to earn money for drugs than stealing or dealing. So they'd hang around the Barb office on Tuesday nights waiting for the paper. Usually no one showed up before eleven, the earliest the papers might be back from the printer, but by midnight, this tremendous mob would be camped out in the street, very weird because, by this time, all the stores were locked up and even the movie theater down the block had put out its lights

"I didn't need to be there when the paper came out, but sometimes I'd have gone to a late movie with the other Barb staffers. We'd walk out of the theater and see hundreds of shadows in the darkness, half-lit by the distant street lamps.

"No one impatient—oh, some might be trying to score off their neighbor, but there were usually enough reds floating around to pacify the most afflicted. Very quiet, that's probably why the cops left us all alone, just a faint rustle in the darkness, like the opening scene in Boris Goudnov where the crowd is waiting in the snow in the square outside St Stephens.

"Anyhow the dopers would get their papers—buy them for a nickel, sell them for a quarter—and then hitchhike off to wherever they lived, San Francisco, Oakland, selling papers along the way. There were three ways you could buy anything back in those days—cash, grass, and Barbs, they were all more or less acceptable legal tender.

"When I think back, we had quite a community going on University Avenue—a regular Penny Lane—the Barb office, the movie theater, the drug store for smokes and pipe tobacco, a couple of your basic cheap-but-good restaurants, to say nothing of the street people who sold things or simply stood or sat in the same place outside the Barb office day after day and looked weird. You knew everybody by the names they gave you. We may have been freaky but we were still predictable.

"Just down the street from the Barb, there was a coffee shop—not one of the ones that anybody from our small town ever went to—I often wonder who did eat inside—cab drivers? buyers from the department stores around the corner on Shattuck? A Gazette vending machine stood outside the restaurant—God knows why—if one of us put a dime in to get a paper we'd lift the entire lot—but maybe the people who ate in the coffee shop paid. The headline about the killing was visible through the front plastic of the vending rack. I'd parked my car two blocks over, where there were no meters, and was walking toward the Barb office planning to use their old typewriters to write up my research notes—those typewriters were real antiques, direct from Mark Twain and Brett Harte to us—when I saw the headline through the clear plastic—Minority Officer Killed.

"Some black scumbags calling themselves the African Liberation Army or something like that—I don't think there were ever more than two in their 'army,' had shot and killed a police officer. 'In the name of the people,' the letter they left on his dashboard proclaimed. Only the officer they killed, Ron Tsukamoto, was a Japanese-American, the first non-Caucasian Berkeley ever had on its police force.

"His killing was a sort of preview of the way things were going to be in California in the 1990's when everyone is a minority and we all hate each other. You know, 'Blacks battle Hispanics at South Gate High,' 'Hispanic Gangs fight with Asians in Westminster.' Coming on top of Altamont, Tsukamoto's killing told me the summer of love was

204

over. 'They offed a pig,' someone said in my presence. 'They killed a police officer,' I replied.

"I got in my automobile, picked up some tanning lotion and headed south. Of course, there being some unused grant money at JPL's Pasadena facility at the time didn't hurt."

"And that's how you met Mom."

"Right. And now here you are."

"Yeah. Here we both are." And I looked at my father in the year of our lord 1997 and wondered what we were both going to do and how we were going to go on from here.

POLICE HUNT FOR COP SLAYER;

CHIEF: KILLING WAS POLITICAL.

He Was a Berkeley Kind of Person

by Lari Blumenfeld

Gazette Staff Writer

"He was a Berkeley kind of a person..."

"He was a gracious quiet easy guy to talk to..."

"He did what he was asked — what he was told to do. He was a good policeman..."

"He was such a sweet guy—never any trouble..."

He was Ronald Tsugio Tsukamoto, 28, born at the
Tule Lake Relocation Center, July 29 1942 and
killed by an assassin's bullet yesterday in the city
he loved while performing a line of duty in which
he deeply believed."

The rest of the article records how Tsukamoto stopped a motorcyclist for making an illegal U-turn. While he and the cyclist were chatting—Tsukamoto never did issue a citation—the assassin walked up to them, pulled a gun from his pocket and fired twice, hitting Tsukamoto in the right eye.

"The gunman fired a second shot that went over Tsukamoto's head and hit a sign across the street. Tsukamoto was already falling forward and toward the ground. The gunman dashed across the street and jumped into the passenger side of a waiting car that had been parked, lights out and engine running.

"A letter claiming responsibility for Tsukamoto's death showed up at the Barb office about an hour later.

"Who cares what it said."

27. Phillip

I last saw my father when I was sixteen. We had a fight or, rather, he fought with me, throwing me to the floor and breaking my collarbone.

My mother had telephoned him and asked him to come to our house and speak to me about my uncooperative attitude. My mother and father had been separated then for almost ten years. My father lost his temper while he was talking with me; he had been losing his temper, slowly, almost since the moment he entered our house—our apartment rather. In the end, his only choices were to love me or to hurt me.

The separation had been responsible for my mother and I moving out of the duplex, the one with the huge back yard we had called home since I was an infant. I'd learned to ski there, swaddled in layers of winter clothing, on a hillside, nearly as tall as I was, that my father had built in the center of our yard. And I'd earned my first nickel there, or was it a dime, by proving to our next-door neighbor that I could be silent for five minutes.

After several months back in the Midwest with my grandparents, after my mother and father first separated, she and I lived in a series of successively smaller apartments, each indistinguishable from a hundred similar apartments in the surrounding corridors. My father lived in an apartment, also. His apartment seemed much grander than ours because it was downtown and on the top floor of a seven-story building. In fact, his apartment was just as shabby as ours, just as confining.

An example: The carpets in the halls of our apartment house were cheap but durable—designed for the frequent comings and goings of unstable tenants and the games of children who will persist in running up and down the halls no matter how often you tell them 'No.' The carpets in the halls and elevators of my father's adults-only building had looked luxurious the day he moved in, but were worn and threadbare within a year or two. My father, of course, never saw the wear and tear or pretended not to see it. My father's life relied on illusions. To see the world as my father saw it, you had to shut out the present in favor of the past, to envision things as they should have been. I can sympathize now with my father's drinking, though I still cannot approve.

As a result of the separation, my family traded that single wonderful house for two confining apartments, just as that one terrible day in September, I traded my father for ten comic books.

"We're going away for awhile," my mother said, "we're going to go back and stay with your grandparents."

At the railway station, I couldn't stop crying. "I want my father," I said.

"If you'll stop crying, I'll buy you something," my mother promised.

"What?" She bought me ten comic books. I traded my father for ten comic books that I'd read through completely before we were out of the train station.

I'd been drinking that evening of the quarrel with my father, a homemade brew of sugar, pineapple juice, and fermented bananas that I'd cooked up just to see if it could be done. For all I knew, it might have contained little or no alcohol, but I sipped at it, trying to turn the sipping into a mature gesture, as though by clutching this tiny fruit glass I could communicate to my father that I, too, was strong and mature, a force to be contended with.

This imposture hadn't worked of course; although my voice had changed the year before, was the deep baritone it is today; somehow, in my father's presence, my voice still seemed reedy and piping. He decided on an impulse to spank me—though by then I was much too large to be picked up and spanked, underweight still, but already an inch taller than my father. Failing to raise me to the desired height across his lap, he hurled me to the floor like an unwanted object.

What had our quarrel been about? That I'd done something I shouldn't have done—broken a window or been rude to my mother. More likely, it was because I'd refused to obey my mother—I'd been on permanent strike for almost two months then, like my own teenage children would be three decades later, and my father had been annoyed by my mother's too frequent phone calls for assistance. This was the key to his anger—my father had never really cared for me—(something that perhaps might have made a spanking tolerable)—he only wanted relief from the phone calls, perpetuation of the illusion that all was going smoothly, that he Peter Freygood was a success.

At that time, years after the divorce, my father had a mistress, the blond, very buxom wife of a big-shot politician. She embodied the perfection—financial and family, that he, poor Jew, spurred on by his father to seize the day, had always reached for and never attained. She also had a son, a year younger than I was; like her, he was all too blond and perfect. I didn't measure up.

"Why can't you be like Randy?" my father had said to me more than once. "Randy is the junior tennis champion at his club."

"I don't play tennis, Dad."

"But I bought you a racket."

You bought me a racket, but you took me to play golf, to be your caddy and, maybe, once or twice, if we were alone on a fairway with no foursome pressing in on us, to let me swing a club. All right, I'll admit it: your disinterest wasn't the only reason I hadn't learned to play tennis. I wasn't much of an athlete; I wasn't coordinated then like Randy. But your offers to help me with golf, to coach me in tennis were desultory, intermittent, uncoordinated also, never there when I wanted, needed them.

After the beating, my father never spoke with me again. Nor did I attempt to contact him. I went to McGill University in Montreal for my first two years of college. My father's apartment was just a ten-minute walk from the McGill campus. But I never went to his apartment, nor did my father and I ever meet for supper or for lunch.

In my Junior year, I transferred to the University of California but I came back to Montreal each summer. Each time I came back, I'd ask about my father and, occasionally, hear that my father had asked after me. But we never telephoned each other, never once the entire time I was home. He never called me during the school year either. He knew where I went to school; he could have called me if he wanted to. But he never wanted to. And I never telephoned him.

After I graduated, my contacts with my family were less frequent. Sometimes, my mother and I would talk on the phone once or twice a week and sometimes six months would go by without my writing to her. She always wrote to me, faithfully, at least once a week, until the year she died, but I would generally put her letters by unread. They always contained the same messages, "You're just like your father," or "your brother wouldn't have turned out this way except for you."   I had my own adult anguish to contend with.

Only much later, after I'd sired Dana, and Donna, and Dina and felt confident in my own marriage was I able to turn to my mother and say, "I'm not like my father," and "My brother must take his own path; I'll help him when I can, but I'm not responsible for him."

It took me almost two years after my father's death to begin to mourn him, and more than ten years before I could finally point to individual traits of his that I admired, to discuss shared experiences, say I liked "this" about him, I disliked "that," and accept that no matter how hard I might long for his love and affection, my father, now dead, could never change, would never love me.

I have written that I have five children, all daughters, but, in fact, until this year, I had none.

Two of my daughters are products of my youth. I barely knew them. One, a love child, I never knew at all. I only met her in a photograph.

I had a girl friend once who told me that when she was eighteen or nineteen, she learned for the first time that she had been adopted. Her parents had just separated, and her mother, distraught, had finally confided in her. Two years later, when she was twenty-one, she decided to track down her biological father. She took a plane to the city where he lived and called him from the airport. "I don't have any money," he said cautiously; it was the very first thing he said to her after she'd identified herself.

"I don't want your money," she screamed into the phone and began to cry.

"Well, uh, tell me about yourself."

She began to tell him, all in a rush, but when she paused for breath, he said, "That's great. Look, next time you're going to be in town, send me a post card."

She cried all the way home on the plane.

I have always anticipated that someday I too would get a phone call from one or both of my two lost children, but the call has never come.

Dana, my eldest daughter from my present marriage, is my inseparable partner in a thousand photographs taken from her birth to the age of eighteen. At nineteen she rejected further intimacy with her family and her friends, contrived quarrels, and has since lived apart from me, her mother, and her sisters. I wish her success and would hug her if I could. I miss her terribly.

My estrangement from Donna, my middle daughter, is so complete that all I have are memories of things we did together, a decade or more ago.

When Donna was—what—nine or ten, we went cross-country skiing in a group—two families—ours and the Varsas. Dana and Paul Varsa's son, Paul Jr., had gone to the first grade together. I knew the area, a county park, where we were to ski well, but the park was near where the Varsas lived, so Paul Varsa was our nominal leader.

Things went well enough at first, a bright, though distant sun that was warm enough if you kept on the move, the scent of pine, a line of paw prints in the snow that may have belonged to a rabbit. I think Kathy (my wife) may have had some uneasy moments, but the trip itself was relatively uneventful until we came to the bend where the trail looped in almost a U. The U had a stubby tail, an alternate path that led over and through a creek. People go that way sometimes in the summer and early fall to pick the berries. And people go there who simply don't know the trail. I made the loop—I was a little ahead of our group—and was surprised a few moments later to find I was still alone on the path. I should have turned back at that point, but I didn't; I felt rejected along with my knowledge of the path in favor of Paul Varsa and struck out at top speed. It was only after twenty minutes had gone by—I'd slowed by then and allowed not one but three parties of skiers to pass me, that I turned back to find my family had taken the wrong turn.

As I suspected, the Varsas had gone on toward the Creek, and Donna, too trusting, had pressed through the soft ice. Her left foot was soaked and wet. The group had decided, sensibly, to turn back but had got confused in their direction. They were lost.

"Why haven't you changed her socks?" I asked. Admittedly, my statement, put in the form of a question, could only make trouble, not resolve it. Yes, I learned to ask such questions from my father; but I'm not my father and my anger is my own.

The day was crisp and cold; the snow melted only if and where the sun struck an exposed patch of earth or a dark branch; otherwise, in the shadow of a cloud, it refroze immediately. I took off my own ski boot—I was wearing two pairs of socks, and removed the outer stocking. Then, I took off my daughter's wet sock and shoe and put my dry sock on her foot in place of her wet one, first using my second sock and the dry hem of my flannel shirt to wick away the moisture from her tiny foot. Her boot was too wet to be replaced, so I simply lifted her up to my shoulders and skied rapidly back toward the house. Her mother followed carrying Donna's skis and the wet boot.

The second memory I have of Donna and I together is of taking her with me on a business trip to Wisconsin.

It was a fun trip in many ways: I remember the excitement in Donna's eyes when we got to the motel. She had our stuff unpacked, out of the suitcases, and into the drawers in imitation of her mother almost as soon as we arrived. I know how to make a house for you, Dad, her actions seemed to be saying. Certainly, her conduct when she was alone with me on the trip was entirely different, more mature, than her behavior at home. If Dana or Dina had been along, Donna might have been fighting for control of the TV or wanting to go down to the lobby to buy postcards, but on that trip, with just the two of us for company, she was infernally adult, all her pleasure coming from the raw experience of being.

I screwed up in the Chicago airport on the way back, though one could blame the incident on the now (and deservedly) defunct Republic Airlines. Who would believe that on a single connecting ticket—Republic from Wisconsin to Chicago, Republic again from Chicago to Kalamazoo, that I would be expected to check in a half hour early on the second leg? But when we got to the departure gate at O'Hare—I'd dawdled between gates and taken the time to get Donna and I a hamburger at an Airport restaurant—I learned we'd been bumped.

"You should have checked in earlier," they said, as if having boarded the plane in Madison we might somehow have vanished in mid air. And what did Republic propose to do about their error? An hotel room? An apology? They put us on a bus, sent us out in a snowstorm around the bottom of Lake Michigan, and told us that in two or three hours, perhaps six if the storm persisted, we might make it home. A disaster? No. For there was my Donna, smiling and agreeable, the perfect companion with which to stare down

214

adversity. I felt so ashamed I had failed her, a long unpleasant bus ride instead of a plane, so ashamed, and yet she thought the bus trip just another part of the continuing adventures of Donna and Dad. I loved her then, fervently; she is a very special person. I do not know where she is today, who she is staying with, or whether she is still in school.

Dina, as my youngest, is the one I know least of all my children. I still have no clear impression of her goals. I see her sometimes as reacting, not responding, and, in consequence, of allowing herself to be manipulated by others. The stronger her protests, the less her will is really her own; she is the captive of a "hidden" script. To be fair, these are impressions of a much younger, still unformed human. I don't know her at all well as she is today.

I know the young child that did not want to go to kindergarten, that came home at noon her second day in first grade on the kindergarteners' bus. But I have made only the barest start at knowing the young woman, almost an adult, who shares my house and my table, the researcher who has begun to study me.

The reality is terrifying: I know all about my father whom I hate; I know nothing about my daughters whom I love.

To purchase more fine books like the one you've read, go to http://zanybooks.com.

www.ingramcontent.com/pod-product-compliance
Lightning Source LLC
Chambersburg PA
CBHW071157260626
47162CB00003B/1083